OCT   2022

Heartwood Hotel

THE GREATEST GIFT

Also by Kallie George

Heartwood Hotel, Book 1: A True Home

The Magical Animal Adoption Agency, Book 1: Clover's Luck

The Magical Animal Adoption Agency, Book 2: The Enchanted Egg

The Magical Animal Adoption Agency, Book 3: The Missing Magic

Heartwood Hotel

THE GREATEST GIFT

Kallie George

illustrated by
Stephanie Graegin

DISNEP • HYPERION
Los Angeles   New York

First Hardcover and Paperback Editions, July 2017
10 9 8 7 6 5 4 3 2
FAC-020093-17293
Printed in the United States of America

This book is set in 15.25 Fournier/Monotype, Qiber/Fontspring
Designed by Phil Caminiti
Illustrations created in pencil

Library of Congress Cataloging-in-Publication Data
Names: George, Kallie, author. • Graegin, Stephanie, illustrator.
Title: The greatest gift / by Kallie George ; illustrated by Stephanie Graegin.
Description: First edition. • Los Angeles ; New York : Disney-Hyperion, [2017] Series:
    The Heartwood hotel ; 2 • Summary: The peaceful winter that Mona the mouse
    expected at the Heartwood Hotel is disturbed by a difficult guest, food shortages
    caused by a huge blizzard, and secrets.
Identifiers: LCCN 2016034310 • ISBN 9781484732342 (hardcover) •
    ISBN 1484732340 (hardcover) • ISBN 9781484746394 (paperback)
Subjects: CYAC: Hotels, motels, etc.—Fiction. Mice—Fiction. Forest animals—
    Fiction. Winter—Fiction.
Classification: LCC PZ7.G293326 Gre 2017 | DDC [Fic]—dc23
LC record available at https://lccn.loc.gov/2016034310

Reinforced binding
Visit www.DisneyBooks.com

To Vikki ♥
—K.G.

For Theresa and Sophia
—S.G.

Contents

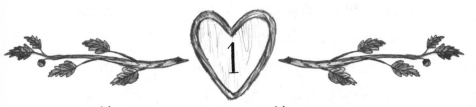

HIBERNATION AT THE HEARTWOOD

Snow fell softly outside the Heartwood Hotel. It was sleepy snow, the kind that took its time to reach the ground. Mona the mouse watched through a small window in the ballroom, leaning against the handle of her dandelion broom. It was so quiet she could almost hear the flakes touch down.

St. Slumber's Supper was finally over. The food was eaten, the music was sung, and gifts were given out by Mr. Heartwood: little sweet-smelling pillows filled with

herbs and lavender, to help the hibernating guests sleep soundly until spring.

And now they had all gone to bed—the groundhog, some toads, turtles, and ladybugs, and so many chipmunks no one could keep track of them.

Even the Higginses, who were hedgehogs, were hibernating. Mr. Higgins was the gardener and Mrs. Higgins was the housekeeper. They weren't needed since only a few non-hibernating guests were booked for the winter months. Most animals in Fernwood Forest, whether they slept through the winter or not, stayed at home.

The Heartwood Hotel was Mona's home now, and she loved it, from the heart carved on the front door to the stargazing balcony on the topmost branches to all of her new friends, like Tilly, the red squirrel maid, and Cybele, the swallow songstress.

Tilly said that the winter season was always really boring, but Mona didn't mind. She had been a maid at the Heartwood only a few months since arriving, wet and afraid, in the fall. But already she had helped save the hotel from wolves and earn it a top review in the *Pinecone Press*. As proud as she was of that, it would be nice to finally rest and roast acorns in the fireplace this winter.

Mona could smell roasted acorns now, their delicious aroma floating up from the kitchen downstairs. The staff was having their own little feast later, and she could hardly wait.

Her stomach grumbled, but she turned her attention back to the task at hand and made a final sweep with her broom, putting the last bits of twine, leftover from the gift-giving, in the dust basket. The twine could be used again, so it would need to be taken to the storage room. But the basket was too full for Mona to lift. She'd have to ask Tilly for help.

Mona was just leaving the ballroom to find the squirrel when she heard a voice in the hallway.

"Ah, shadow, what's that you say? A toast to

you? Yes, of course! A toast." There was a pause, then a gulping, smacking sound, followed by a happy sigh.

Mona recognized the voice. It was the groundhog, Mr. Gibson. He was supposed to be in bed!

She found him just outside the ballroom, staring at his shadow on the wall.

"Mr. Gibson, can I help you?" asked Mona.

"Oh! Is the party over?" The groundhog turned around. He was holding a small sweet-smelling pillow in one paw and a cup in another. His nose was shiny and sticky with honey.

"Yes," said Mona. "It finished a while ago. But if you're still hungry, I can find you something to eat." She knew how important it was that the hibernators were well fed.

"So kind of you. The staff at the Heartwood is always so thoughtful. You even gave us gifts." He shook the lavender pillow. "But no, I am stuffed," he said, patting his stomach. "Even my shadow is full." He chuckled, then gave a big yawn. Before Mona knew it, he'd fallen asleep right on his feet!

Mona smiled and leaned her broom against the wall. "Come on," she said, gently waking him. "Let's get you to bed."

"Ah, so kind, so kind," replied Mr. Gibson.

The groundhog trundled sleepily after Mona, down the hallway, through the lobby, to the stairs. He kept on mumbling to himself, "Ah, shadow, come along, too. Bed for both of us."

His shadow, and Mona's too, did follow them down the staircase, bobbing on the wall in the light cast by the glowworms.

Down, down, down Mona and Mr. Gibson went, past the kitchen, laundry, and staff bedrooms to the suites deep underground, nestled between the Heartwood's roots.

The hallway was darker here, earthy and cool.

There were special vents that carried air from outside to keep the rooms just the right temperature. Too cold and the guests wouldn't be able to sleep. Too warm and they might think it was spring and wake up early.

No one sounded awake now. Snoring—from squeaky to rumbling—echoed down the passage. Mona led Mr. Gibson down the hall, past the storage room, then doors big and small, all closed. Hanging on each doorknob was a sign: DO NOT DISTURB TILL THE DEWS.

Except for Mr. Gibson's doorknob, where the sign was flipped the other way: I'M AWAKE. PLEASE TIDY MY ROOM.

Mona led him inside.

A lantern softly lit the room, which was sparsely decorated save for pictures of sleeping animals on the walls. Like all the hibernation suites, the bed took up most of it. This one had been specially

prepared for the groundhog and was made of sweet-smelling dried grasses.

"Thank you," said Mr. Gibson, with another yawn, as he undid his tie. He lay down on the bed and, right away, seemed to fall asleep.

"No problem," whispered Mona. "Happy hibernation, Mr. Gibson. Rest well."

She was about to leave, taking the lantern with her, when the groundhog sat bolt upright.

"SHADOW!" he cried.

Mona jumped.

The groundhog's ears were pricked, his eyes wide.

"Mr. Gibson, what's wrong?"

But he didn't seem to hear her. "Shadow!" he cried again, shaking his paw in the air. There was no shadow anywhere to be seen, but Mr. Gibson kept crying, "Shadow, oh, shadow. This is a bad sign. This is bad, bad. . . ."

"What do you mean? What's bad, Mr. Gibson?"

 8

She tried to keep her voice calm, but her heart was racing.

"Danger!" cried the groundhog, though Mona couldn't tell if he was answering her or still speaking to his invisible shadow. "Danger rises," he continued. "It rises outside and it creeps within."

"What do you mean?" Mona asked again, her heart beating even faster now.

But Mr. Gibson didn't reply.

Instead, after a long moment, he fell back against the bed. "Shadow, shadow, shadow," he murmured, but the edge was gone from his voice. He gave an enormous yawn, and with that, pulled the blanket over him, closed his eyes, and began to snore.

Mona's tail was trembling as she tiptoed out of his room, shutting the door quietly behind her and flipping the sign. Mr. Gibson's sign was the only one that read PLEASE WAKE EARLY FOR SHADOW-SPOTTING.

Back in the hallway, she took a deep breath.

She was probably overreacting. Surely, there was no danger here. "Sleep in safety, eat in earnest, and be happy at the Heartwood." That was one of the hotel's many mottos.

Even so, Mona hurried to tell Mr. Heartwood the groundhog's grave, and peculiar, prediction.

The St. Slumber Supper

It was time for the staff's supper, so Mona hurried to the kitchen, hoping to find Mr. Heartwood there to tell him about the groundhog's warning.

But when Mona walked into the kitchen, all thoughts of the groundhog and his prediction left her head. She knew about the special supper—but she hadn't expected the kitchen to be decorated so nicely. It was almost as fancy as the dining hall upstairs!

Hanging from the roots on the ceiling, between the baskets and pots, were bright red holly berries and spiderwebs shaped like snowflakes. The cupboards, dug into the dirt walls, were also framed with festive berries. And on the wall there hung a large calendar that read DAYS TILL THE DEWS with a picture of a spring flower on the last square. Although delicious smells filled the air, there were no platters laid out on the table. Instead it was heaped with packages wrapped in brown paper and tied with brightly colored twine. There were even packages piled up in the shell sink!

All the staff was gathered around the table: Ms. Prickles, the porcupine cook; Gilles, the front-desk lizard; the laundry rabbits, Maggie and Maurice; and Tilly and Cybele, of course. Standing at the head of the table was Mr. Heartwood himself, a big badger and the owner of the Heartwood. Usually he wore a tie and a ring of keys hung from his neck, but not tonight. Tonight he was dressed very strangely indeed.

"Ooo, there you are, Mona," said Tilly. "Sit here! Doesn't Mr. Heartwood look great?"

"Why is he wearing his pajamas?" asked Mona in a whisper, as she took a seat beside the red squirrel.

"Those aren't pajamas." Tilly laughed. "He's dressed like St. Slumber. You know!"

Mona shook her head. "I didn't know there actually was a St. Slumber. I thought it was just the name of the hibernators' feast."

"Oh no," said Tilly, looking surprised. "Your mom and dad *must* have told you about St. Slumber. . . ." She stopped herself. Mona's parents had lost their lives in a storm when she was just a mouseling. She had lived alone in Fernwood Forest for as long as she could remember, before finding the Heartwood. Tilly, too, had lost her family. Although Tilly's loss was more recent—and to coyotes, not a storm—being on their own was something they shared.

"Oh, I'm sorry," said Tilly, reaching for Mona's paw and giving it a squeeze. "Well, St. Slumber is a . . ." She paused. "Actually—no one really can agree on what animal he was. Mr. Heartwood says he was a badger. Although I'm pretty sure he was a red squirrel. That's what my mom said."

"What did he do?" asked Mona.

"The story goes that he was the one who gave us animals our gifts. Thick fur to stay warm, big bellies to hold lots of food, and strong noses to smell food under snow. You know, all the things to help us make it through the winter. We always have a St. Slumber supper at the Heartwood to celebrate."

"But where's the food?"

"Gifts first, food after," said Tilly.

"Gifts?" asked Mona.

"These are all gifts, of course," Tilly replied. "You know! I've been talking about them *all* week."

"I thought you meant the lavender pillows," said Mona.

"The gifts we made for the guests? Oh no," said Tilly. "*These* are the gifts to get excited about!" Tilly picked up one of the packages from the pile in front of her and gave it an inquisitive shake. She didn't have a chance to explain further, however, because Mr. Heartwood cleared his throat, and everyone went quiet.

"St. Slumber's way is the best, to start a season of calm and rest. Let's give gifts to show we care, to keep us happy till skies turn fair." Mr. Heartwood always spoke like this, and Mona was growing used to it. "Now, go to!" he added, spreading his arms wide.

Tilly didn't hesitate. She eagerly tore open the package she was holding. "Oh! My favorite! Roasted acorn cake! Thanks, Ms. Prickles," she called to the porcupine across the table.

"You're welcome, dearie," Ms. Prickles called back. She, too, was opening a gift, using a quill to snap the twine around a box. Mona watched as she pulled out a spoon carved from a seedpod. "Mr. Heartwood, it's lovely!" she exclaimed.

All around the table, the animals were opening presents and smiling. Cybele was thanking Maggie and Maurice for a package of blank bark—"To write your songs on," they said—while Gilles was tasting a colorful concoction of berries wrapped in leaves. "It's a recipe from the tropics that a guest gave to me. I had to improvise with the ingredients a bit," Ms. Prickles told him. "But don't eat too much now. We have a feast coming."

Everyone looked so happy.

"Aren't you going to open your gifts, too?" Tilly asked Mona.

"My gifts?"

Tilly pointed to a stack of packages heaped up in front of Mona. "Those ones are for you."

Mona couldn't believe it. She had never gotten a gift before. The only thing she could remember being given was the key from Mr. Heartwood, for the rooms. Though that wasn't really a gift, but something she'd earned. Now, though, she had a whole pile of them!

"Come on! Start with this one!" Tilly handed her a small box wrapped in brown paper and tied up with twine. "I can't wait till you see what it is!"

FROM TILLY & MRS. HIGGINS read a tag made from a piece of bark. Slowly Mona undid the twine and removed the paper. Inside the box was an apron, with a tiny lopsided heart sewn on the front pocket.

"I thought it was about time you had an apron your size," said Tilly. It was true. Mona's current apron was meant for a squirrel, not a mouse, and she often tripped over it.

"Mrs. Higgins made it, but I sewed on the heart," continued Tilly proudly.

"It's . . . it's . . ." It was perfect, lopsided heart and everything, but Mona couldn't get the words out.

"I *knew* you'd like it." Tilly grinned.

Mona started to put it on, but Tilly said, "No, no, try it on later. You'd better keep opening, before supper starts. Me too!"

And so, Mona did. There was cheese crumble covered in blueberry sauce from Ms. Prickles, and a rolled-up piece of bark from Cybele.

Heartwood Hotel, Heartwood Hotel, Where feathered and furred together can dwell...

It was the song the swallow had written, the one she sang for Mona when they first became friends.

Even Gilles had given her something—her very own subscription to the *Pinecone Press*. "So I don't catch you reading the hotel's copy. That's meant for the guests only," he explained, but Mona was sure she saw a twinkle in his eye.

When Mona had unwrapped the last package

in her pile, Mr. Heartwood came over and set a VERY large present in front of her, which wasn't wrapped, perhaps because of its size.

It was a walnut case, like the one she had lost in the fall, running from the wolves. Except that case had belonged to her parents, and her father had carved a heart into it. This one had clasps in the shape of hearts instead.

"This cannot replace the one you lost," Mr. Heartwood said, "nor is it a case with which to roam. It's a place for you to store your things, now that the Heartwood is your home."

Mona gasped. It was beautiful, polished to perfection, and it even smelled good—rich and nutty and sweet.

"Oh, OH! Thank you!" she said. It didn't feel like enough. But she had nothing to give him back, nothing to give anyone.

Mr. Heartwood, however, just waved his paw.

"Gifts are done. Back to your seats. It's time at last for us to eat!"

Though Mona tried to enjoy the special St. Slumber Supper, her thoughts kept wandering back to the gifts. She had never owned so many beautiful things. If only she'd known. She would have given gifts to everyone. She hoped they knew that.

Later, in her room that she shared with Tilly, she placed each gift carefully in her new case. Except for her apron, which she played with, tying and retying the string into different bows.

"That's just what my brother used to do. But instead of playing with his gifts, he'd play with all the wrapping. He was really little. I wish . . ." Tilly looked sad for a moment.

Mona wasn't sure what to say, so instead she draped her apron over her chair to wear the next day.

Then Tilly took a big munch of her acorn cake and asked, "Do you like your gifts?"

"Like them? I love them," said Mona. "But . . ."

"But what?"

"I didn't get Ms. Prickles or Cybele or Mr. Heartwood anything. I didn't get *you* anything. . . . I didn't realize. . . ."

"I thought you knew about St. Slumber, otherwise I would have told you," said Tilly. "It's not a rule or anything. But everyone *always* exchanges gifts."

Mona felt her stomach sink. *"Always?"*

Tilly shrugged. "You didn't know. It doesn't *really* matter."

Still, Mona climbed into bed, worrying. Even if Tilly seemed to understand, what about the others?

I need *to get everyone a gift,* she decided. *But what?* She wasn't a songstress, like Cybele. Or a cook, like Ms. Prickles. She didn't have anyone to work with, like Tilly and Mrs. Higgins. She *was* good at ideas though. She would think of something.

And with that comforting thought, Mona eventually fell asleep to dreams of a mouse dressed in pajamas and a cap, carrying a walnut case with a heart on it, filled with presents.

THE ROYAL RABBIT

In the morning, it was still snowing—harder now—and Mona remembered the groundhog's warning.

She told Mr. Heartwood about it at breakfast, but he only laughed. "Grave is a groundhog, with a head half in fog. Predict they might, but they are rarely right. That's what my grandfather used to say. Don't listen to all their warnings. Besides," said Mr. Heartwood, "we have plenty of food, which is all one needs for a happy winter."

"Except for cheese," said Ms. Prickles, who was

stirring a pot of soup on the stove with her new spoon. "There's none left in the storage room. We must have eaten more than I thought last night."

"I'll order some from the Squirrels' Delivery Service," said Gilles. Now that Mrs. Higgins was sleeping, he was taking over more of the house-keeping duties, along with his usual front-desk ones. "We'll need plenty for when the hibernators wake."

"The Squirrels' Delivery Service?" Mona whispered to Tilly.

"The biggest storage and delivery service in all of Fernwood," Tilly explained.

Gilles went on: "We *do* have certain standards to uphold, after all. Even if there aren't any new guests booked. Of course, the carpenter ants are coming. They're expected today, to begin work on the new insect-sized suites."

"Yes, that is what the winter is for, rest and

renovation, as all the guests snore," said Mr. Heartwood. "And speaking of snoring, I myself am going to take a nap today." This wasn't surprising. After all, Mr. Heartwood was a badger. And, though badgers weren't true hibernators, they were extra sleepy in winter. "I'm sure you will be able to handle anything that comes your way."

Mona was sure, too. After all, Tilly had said that nothing exciting happened in winter.

Certainly nothing exciting happened that morning. There was even time for Gilles to frame and hang a copy of the *Pinecone Press* review—and polish the frame three times! Soon enough, it was early afternoon. All the rooms were clean, and Mona had just finished sweeping snow off the branch balconies. Chilled, she was taking a brief break to warm herself by the lobby fire and dry her new apron, which had gotten damp from the flakes.

Her apron really *was* perfect. Not only did it fit just right, the heart looked remarkably like the one on the Heartwood door. She needed to think of a gift as nice for Tilly, for everyone. She was in the middle of pondering when the front door opened.

Whoosh! In came a rush of snow and with it a rabbit, as white and fluffy as the flurries themselves. She was wearing a glittery scarf, neatly wrapped around her neck. In one gloved paw, she held a cane, which she tapped on the moss rug. Then she surveyed the lobby with a haughty sniff.

"Humph. So *this* is the Heartwood."

She sniffed again. "I knew I would be disappointed. I really should stop reading that *Pinecone Press*. It always *does* exaggerate." She tapped her cane on the rug again.

"This *is* the Heartwood," piped Mona, jumping up, smoothing her apron, and hurrying over.

"A maid who sits by the fireplace instead of

working? My, my," said the rabbit, clucking her tongue. "In my warren, such a thing is not tolerated."

Mona's cheeks flushed. "Can I help you, Ms. . . . ?"

"It is not Ms., or Mrs., or Miss. It is *Duchess*, Duchess Hazeline." She paused. "Surely you have heard of me?"

"Actually, no, I . . ." Mona started.

The Duchess sniffed again. "Really, what *do* mice teach their young nowadays?"

Before Mona could say anything about being on her own, the Duchess interrupted again. "Yes, well. Suffice it to say, I am from rabbit royalty. I was on my way to a very important conference. But the snow has hindered me. I can't stay out in it for long, or I get a terrible chill. My old coat is simply not as thick as it used to be."

"You don't look that old," said Mona, regretting the words the moment they left her mouth.

"You are trying to flatter me," the Duchess said, with another sniff. "I *am* old—that's a fact. I hope it's a fact, too, that this IS a five-acorn establishment."

"It is," assured Mona, quickly, feeling more and more out of her depth.

"Very well then. I will take the most luxurious accommodations you offer, until the snow passes. Which I hope will be soon. My friends are already going to be terribly disappointed that I am late."

"The penthouse is our best room," said Mona.

"Then book me in at once," the Duchess demanded, impatiently tapping her cane on the rug again.

Mona hesitated. She had run into trouble before while booking a guest by herself. "I just need to fetch Gilles. . . ."

The Duchess didn't let her finish. "I cannot believe this!" The rabbit's voice rose shrilly, and Mona felt sure this exchange wouldn't end well.

"*SHHH!*" came a voice from behind them.

To Mona's relief, Gilles emerged from the main office. "Mr. Heartwood is trying to sleep," he said.

Upon seeing the rabbit, he stopped in his tracks. Then, with a composure he had perfected, Gilles straightened his bow tie and strode over. "Duchess Hazeline"—he bowed—"most respected of all rabbit royalty, to what do we owe this great honor?"

"Yes, well." The Duchess sniffed again. "I would like to book the penthouse, at once."

"Of course, of course," said Gilles. "Do you have any special requests to make your stay more pleasant, Duchess?"

"Just a few trifles," said the Duchess. Mona listened closely. "My sleigh is outside with my things. I would like them all unpacked. I am allergic to common grasses, so please make sure my bed is only feather or imported grass. I would like a bath drawn, too."

"Of course," said Gilles again.

 31

Mona thought Duchess Hazeline *must* be finished, but she went on: "I want tea and acorn crumpets ready for me. Not covered with jellies or honey, mind. And three bowls of soup: mushroom, peppercorn, and carrot. I am not sure which I am in the mood for."

"That is no problem. Our cook, Ms. Prickles, makes the most delicious soups," said Gilles. "Now, why don't you warm yourself by the fire while we prepare everything?"

"Very well," she said. Then she added, "Oh, and one last thing. My paws are very sensitive. I must have carpet covering the floor. In fact, I like this one." She tapped the lobby's rug with her cane.

"Oh . . ." Gilles faltered for the first time. And Mona could see why.

The rug was an important part of the lobby. It was made from tree moss, a beautiful minty green, and it was the first thing you saw when you came into the Heartwood.

"Surely that isn't a problem?" said the Duchess. "Why, it's only a rug, and not even as nice as the ones in my burrow."

"Yes, yes," said Gilles quickly. "I will just need to wake Mr. Heartwood and ask him. . . ."

"Ask me what, Gilles?" Mr. Heartwood himself emerged from the office, rubbing his eyes. The fur on one side of his nose was pushed flat.

"I—it's . . ." stammered Gilles, gesturing to the Duchess, who was tapping her cane furiously.

"Ah, Duchess Hazeline," said Mr. Heartwood, though he did not look as impressed as Gilles had. He simply nodded and smiled. "What may we do for you?"

The Duchess sniffed, as though waiting for someone else to explain, and Gilles said quickly, quietly, "She would like the rug in her room, Mr. Heartwood, the lobby one."

"Of course she would. And she shall have it. Now, dear Duchess, why don't you rest yourself by the fire, and let me fetch you some hot honey."

"Humph," muttered the Duchess. "It is about time. Not too hot, mind. I have a very sensitive stomach."

The Duchess strode over to one of the couches and took a seat. While Gilles hurried to the front desk to fill out the paperwork, Mr. Heartwood turned to Mona.

"Mona, go on. Do all in your might to make sure the Duchess is treated right."

"Of course, Mr. Heartwood," she replied. So much for a quiet day of gift-planning. They had a guest—the grandest guest Mona had met yet. As difficult as the royal rabbit seemed, she *was* a Duchess, and Mona couldn't help but feel a little excited.

4

THE CHEESE CRUMBLE

"Who eats dry crumpets?" said Ms. Prickles, when Mona relayed the rabbit's requests. "And three soups! Three! I only have one on the menu for tonight. Which means two will go to waste. I can't make just a cup of soup, you know, dearie. Soup takes a pot." She shook her head. With a heavy sigh, she turned to the kitchen cupboards to begin.

Tilly's response was the opposite, her tail bristling with energy. "A duchess! A real duchess! I wish I had been there! We have to make sure everything is perfect. Why didn't you make a list, Mona?"

"I couldn't," said Mona. "She just started talking. There was no time!"

Tilly humphed. "Well, let's hope you remember everything."

And so they scurried to work, too, collecting what they needed from the supply room, then heading upstairs.

The Heartwood Hotel was big—*really* big—but Mona was finally getting to know her way around. On the main floor there were the lobby, ballroom, and dining room. The staircase wound its way up and around the center of the tree. The second floor had a games room, salon, and library for all the guests' enjoyment, but the rest of the floors were designated for different types of guests: the trunk floor for bigger animals, the branch floors mostly for squirrels and rabbits, the twig floors for birds. At the top of the tree were the stargazing balcony and the most expensive rooms: the honeymoon and penthouse suites.

Mona had prepared the honeymoon suite before, for the Sudsburys, a skunk couple who came every fall. And she'd booked Juniper, the June bug and hotel reviewer for the *Pinecone Press*, into the penthouse. Mona had been in charge of meeting the tiny June bug's special requests, such as extra pillows and stepladders, but she hadn't actually gotten the room ready.

This was her first time.

Every Heartwood room was grand. Even the staff bedroom she shared with Tilly was far nicer than anything Mona had ever had before coming to the hotel. But the penthouse was glorious!

The bedroom was enormous, almost as big as the lobby, with a giant bed and walk-in closet, and the bathroom had not only a tub, but its own fur-dryer. Besides the bedroom and bathroom, there was a dining room, with a table and a bar that had

a huge jug set up next to a sign that read HELP YOUR-
SELF. HONEY FLOWS AT THE HEARTWOOD; and a living
room with a twig couch, bookshelf, and fireplace.

A balcony, with a railing carved to look like a
ribbon of leaves, wrapped halfway around the tree.
At one end, there was a perch for messenger jays.
No other guests had private postal service!

As much as Mona wanted to linger and explore
the beautiful suite, they had work to do. Mona and
Tilly laid out the fancy bedding, drew a bath, and
started the fire. Then, while Tilly took care of the
food, Mona began unpacking the Duchess's things.

The Duchess had six cases, which Gilles had
brought upstairs, filled with more clothes and jew-
elry and soft-bark purses than Mona had ever seen.
Things like these would make nice gifts, thought

Mona. *Not for Mr. Heartwood, but Tilly would probably like a purse of her own.*

Tilly! Mona looked up and noticed the squirrel
was talking to her.

"Sorry, Tilly. What did you say?"

Tilly rolled her eyes. "Were you even listening
to me? I asked, is that it? Was there anything else
the Duchess wanted?"

There was! Mona had almost forgotten to fetch
the rug from the lobby. Tilly finished hanging
up the scarves, and Mona dragged the rug up the
stairs. She arranged it in the middle of the room.

At last, everything was in place.

"You can go now, Mona. I'll show the Duchess
up to her room," said Tilly. "I've been here longer,

after all. I have more experience with these kinds of guests."

Mona didn't mind. She was sure the Duchess didn't like her, and she doubted she could do anything to change that.

Down in the kitchen, Ms. Prickles served Mona a bowl of leftover soup. The laundry rabbits were there, too, eating soup and gossiping.

"She has the largest warren in Fernwood Forest," said Maurice.

"My cousin worked for her once," said the other rabbit, Maggie. "There are hundreds of rooms, and all of them are empty. But the Duchess made her clean them every day!"

"It *is* odd that no staff came with her. No one was even pulling her sleigh," continued Maurice. "It's a mystery. But who are we to question a duchess?"

Just then, Tilly burst into the kitchen and thumped down at the table.

"Duchess or no, I am NOT going back up there," she cried. "She's ridiculous! I know Mr. Heartwood would never let us growl at a guest—but sometimes I think we *should* be allowed."

"What happened?" asked Mona.

"She didn't want soup. She didn't want crumpets. She demanded crumble! Cheese crumble. At once!" Tilly's tail bristled. "She even threatened to write a letter of complaint to the *Pinecone Press*!"

Ms. Prickles shook her head. "Oh dear. I don't have any cheese left. I know that Gilles put an order in with the Squirrels' Delivery Service, but that won't arrive for weeks. Chestnut crumble is nice—but I'm in short supply of chestnuts, too. I just don't understand it. We should have plenty." Ms. Prickles shook her head again.

"Like I said, I am NOT going back up there. Mona, YOU tell the Duchess. Good luck," she added, rolling her eyes.

Mona didn't need luck. *What I need is crumble,*

she thought as she headed out of the kitchen.

And then, with a start, she realized *she* had some! The crumble Ms. Prickles had given her last night. She didn't want to give it to the royal rabbit. But she didn't want the royal rabbit to write to the *Pinecone Press*, either. They had worked so hard for their good reputation, and their five-acorn rating. Could the royal rabbit ruin that?

So Mona hurried to her room and got the box. Passing through the lobby, she saw the carpenter ants had arrived in a troop, with lots of tiny saws and hammers. Gilles had gathered them around the table to discuss plans (though they seemed more interested in showing off their strength and kept lifting up vari-ous armchairs).

But Mona couldn't dawdle. She hurried upstairs, knocking on the door. "Come in," she heard the Duchess call from within.

Mona smoothed her apron and pushed the door open.

Duchess Hazeline was lying on the bed, with an eye mask on.

"I have your crumble, Duchess," said Mona.

"Set it on the table," said the rabbit, with a wave of her paw. Mona was about to do so, when the Duchess sat up, peeling up her mask. "Just a moment. There have been too many mishaps here already. I would like to examine that."

The Duchess rose out of bed and strode suspiciously over. She opened the box in Mona's paws and inhaled deeply.

"See, cheese crumble," said Mona. "With blueberry sauce."

"See?" The Duchess's eyes narrowed. "See, indeed!" She snatched a card tucked in the corner of the box. "What is this?"

"I d-don't know," stammered Mona, truthfully.

The Duchess peered at it, her nose twitching

furiously. " 'From Ms. Prickles, to Mona,' it says."
Her eyes flashed almost as scarily as a wolf's!

"Oh!" Mona had only glanced into the box. She
hadn't seen the card.

"Don't tell me this crumble was meant for
you?"

Slowly, Mona nodded.

"You cannot really expect me to eat a gift that
has been already given?" she scoffed. "I have . . . I
have had enough! I will be writing to the *Pinecone
Press* at once!" The Duchess dramatically flung
out a ringed paw, hitting the box of crumble. It
flew right out of Mona's paws
and landed—upside down—on
the floor. Not the floor, actually, but the rug. The beautiful
Heartwood rug.

SPLAT!

Blueberries and cheese went everywhere.

Mona felt her cheeks redden. That was *her* gift, and she hadn't wanted to give it away in the first place. She hadn't known there were rules about gifts. Gifts were a lot more complicated than she thought.

She couldn't stop herself. "If you have to," said Mona, "you can. But I'm really sorry. I didn't know. Just because *you've* had lots of gifts doesn't mean everyone has. My parents died when I was young. I've never had gifts before. Not until now."

Immediately, Mona gulped. She knew she wasn't supposed to talk back to guests—especially a guest like the Duchess. It was one of the Heartwood's most important rules. Now the Duchess would surely write a complaint.

But, to her surprise, the Duchess remained calm. "Humph," she said instead. "How little you know." Then she straightened her posture and waved a paw. "I must rest now. I am tired. I don't think I am hungry after all. Take that away, and we will say no more of it."

And so, Mona picked up one corner of the rug and dragged it out the door, relieved that the Duchess wouldn't be complaining.

But the rug—the beautiful Heartwood rug—was ruined.

Mona knew that there was no way to get out the blueberry stains. And a stained rug just wouldn't do at the Heartwood. Now there would be nothing to grace the floor of the lobby. No rug for guests to dry their feet, or to welcome in animals from the cold. Unless . . .

Suddenly, Mona had an idea.

THE SNOW-SCULPTING

Like the first spring flower poking out from the snow, there is nothing quite as wonderful as a new idea. The Heartwood Hotel needed a rug for their lobby. Mona could make one.

Her father had been good with his paws, she knew that. He had carved the heart on the front door of the hotel. Her mother had been good with her paws, too: she could bake seedcakes as tasty as Ms. Prickles's. Mona had once made a small mat to dry her feet on when she had lived in a particularly damp stump, but nothing as big as a rug. Still, she could see it now: a rug shaped like a heart, made with colorful twine—a bright welcome to all who entered the hotel. And she knew just where to find the twine. There was lots leftover from the gift-giving. She couldn't wait to get started.

Yet it seemed she would have to wait.

Because after supper, Tilly came into their room with a dish of leftover acorn soufflé and two forks. "I heard about the rug," she said. "That Duchess! Now there'll be no rug in the lobby—and lots of extra work, cleaning all the snowy pawprints. It'll probably be spring before we get a new one!"

It'll be sooner than that, thought Mona. She was tempted to tell Tilly her idea, but stopped herself. After all, gifts were supposed to be surprises. She knew that much.

Instead, she shared everything that had happened that day, and they spent the rest of the night discussing the Duchess and eating till they were stuffed.

That was a really nice thing about Tilly. She was as good at listening as she was at grumping.

I'll start the rug tomorrow, thought Mona when at last she snuggled into her bed. *Tomorrow there'll be lots of time.*

But she was wrong. The next day was even busier. And the next.

Even the snow hadn't stopped new guests from arriving. At first it was rabbits, who, upon hearing the Duchess was staying there, decided to check in, too. And then a band of birds arrived. Not a flock, but a band, called the Dove Tones. They had flown all the way from the city for a winter retreat. Before Mona could blink, a whole week was crossed off on the Days till the Dews calendar.

"A special activity is what we need—a sculpting contest in the snow," Mr. Heartwood said one lunchtime, "to keep spirits high—and the noise inside low."

"Are you worried about the hibernators waking up?" asked Mona.

Mr. Heartwood shook his head. "No, no. The suites are deep underground, and temperature, not noise, is key. But *I* could use a nap or two." He sighed, and his sigh became a yawn. "Even a night of fun would do." He yawned again, then was suddenly whisked away by Ms. Prickles, who began to speak to him in a hurried hush.

Mona turned to Tilly. "A sculpting contest! It's so exciting," she said, while she buttered a beechnut biscuit.

"Sounds like a lot of work, that's what," replied Tilly. "We've never done anything like this in the winter. At least not as long as I can remember. It's always been too quiet."

Still, Mona liked the preparing. That afternoon,

she and Tilly bundled up and headed to the courtyard.

In the fall, Mr. Higgins fought a constant battle with the leaves, keeping the colorful clutter raked up. But now the courtyard was all white and smooth, the way a bed looked in the Heartwood when the sheets were tugged tight. The snow had covered all the plants except for the tops of a few bushes and the tall blackberry-vine walls, on which they hung lanterns.

Together they stomped down areas for guests to build their sculptures, and beside each station they placed baskets filled with pretty things to decorate the sculptures, including holly berries and twigs, moss and polished nutshells, and even shiny pebbles. Then Mona helped Tilly shovel a path between each station and pile up the snow for the guests to build with.

Last, they swept some of the snow from the

frozen pond in front of the hotel, in case anyone wanted to go for a skate.

"Have you ever skated before?" asked Tilly.

Mona started to shake her head, but then she remembered when she and Tilly had tied rags to their paws to clean the ballroom floor. "Was it like that?" she asked Tilly, after reminding her.

"Sort of," said Tilly. "But that was more slipping. Not *really* skating. Skating takes lots of practice. I skated at Fernwood Pond with my family when I was little. I'll show you later if you want."

"I'd love you to," said Mona.

"Good," said Tilly. "It's about time we had some fun."

The snow-sculpting night *was* fun. Cybele sang, while the guests worked on their sculptures: snow bunnies with holly-berry eyes and carrot ears, and snow squirrels with small snowball tails. Even the doves made a beautiful snow bird, indented into the snow, marking its outline with tiny polished pebbles. Mona got to see them all as she passed out dishes of hot crab apple pudding and cups of spiced tea.

The only guest not working on a sculpture was the Duchess. She stood alone, under a sparkling snow umbrella, complaining and criticizing everything, even the giant snow bunnies that were clearly being made in her honor.

"I don't see why she doesn't go back inside if she hates it so much," muttered Tilly, coming up behind Mona.

Mona wasn't sure either. Maybe the Duchess was just stubborn. Or maybe it was something else. Mona remembered the Duchess questioning how much she actually knew about her, which really wasn't much at all. Maybe the Duchess had a secret.

Mona turned to Tilly to say so when she noticed a basket full of candied bark in Tilly's paws.

 53

"Are those more gifts?" asked Mona, trying to keep the worry out of her voice.

"Yes," Tilly said. "They're for everyone who entered the contest. Mr. Heartwood doesn't like to choose favorites. He asked me to go fetch these. He must be almost ready to hand them out."

With that, Tilly hurried off to Mr. Heartwood, who was examining a sculpture at the far end of the courtyard.

More gifts—and Mona hadn't even started hers! She still needed to fetch the twine. But when? And then she realized—now was perfect. She was alone, and everyone was busy. The crab apple pudding was gone, and the guests were anxiously waiting for Mr. Heartwood to see their sculptures. No one would miss her, not for a moment. Plus she needed to take in the dishes anyway.

And so, she piled them up on a tray and hurried back into the Heartwood, her head lost in visions of her gift.

The hotel felt empty. Everyone was outside, except a few guests who were warming themselves by the fire. Mona gave them a friendly nod, then scampered down the stairs. The kitchen was quiet, too, except for a pot bubbling over the fireplace. But it was a mess. It seemed like Ms. Prickles had opened every cupboard and pulled everything out. *She must have been looking for something,* thought Mona, as she did a quick clean and made space on the table for the dishes.

At last, she headed to the staircase. When she reached the hibernation hall, she tiptoed, even though the snores were much louder now, and she didn't have far to go.

Around the first corner was the storage room. She'd passed it many times, especially when preparing the hibernation suites, but had never been inside.

Now, after plucking the lantern from the hook on the wall, she slipped in. There was no door, only a curtain draped across the doorway.

Perhaps because, unlike the other rooms in the Heartwood, the storage room was nothing special. The walls were rubbly and undecorated, the floor rough, and the ceiling bare except for a cluster of roots, from which hung a few bunches of herbs.

It was a just a plain old burrow, filled with boxes and crates and bags, in rather messy rows, with labels like BEECHNUT BISCUITS, DRIED MUSHROOMS, and ACORN FLOUR. But the room was cool, and did smell good, rich, and nutty. There were also some lawn chairs and a pile of pillows, extras for the hibernation suites.

And there, beside the pillows: twine. Three whole baskets of it!

Mona was just looking for a place to hang the lantern when she heard a noise.

A scratching, a *scritch-scritch-scratching.* The sound of footsteps, clawed ones, in the dark!

Mona froze and held her breath. Who would be in the storage room in the dark? Certainly not Ms.

Prickles or Mr. Heartwood. Her ears perked, listening, but there were no more sounds. She held up the lantern and stared down the rows of food: the stacks of seeds and roots, bags of dried berries and mushrooms. She didn't see anything. Nothing scampered; nothing scurried.

"Hello?" she called out. There was no answer.

"Hello?" she called out again.

"Mona?"

Mona jumped. She turned to face Tilly, standing in the doorway.

"There you are!" Tilly said. "I've been looking everywhere for you. What are you doing here?"

Mona wasn't sure what to say. She didn't want to tell about the twine. Not yet, at least. She wanted the gift to be a surprise.

Luckily Tilly was distracted. "I thought we were going to skate together."

"Oh!" said Mona. "I forgot, I was . . ."

Tilly humphed.

"Doesn't matter now. The Duchess needs you. She wants some honey cakes. I was going to fetch them, but you can do it instead."

Mona nodded quickly. "We can skate after."

"It'll be too late," said Tilly. And she strode off, muttering, "I guess skating wasn't *that* important."

Mona felt bad. For a moment she wondered about rushing after Tilly and telling her why she was in the storage room. But she hadn't even started the gift, and telling Tilly would ruin it. So she stopped herself and instead turned to find the honey cakes. If she hurried, she'd still have time to fetch the twine, too.

There was no time, however, to worry about the noise she'd heard in the shadows. Besides, it was probably just her imagination.

THE MORNING MEETING

Now Mona could begin working on the rug in earnest. She made a loom out of sticks, and every morning she got up early, before Tilly, to work on it, and every night she told Tilly she was too tired for their usual talks. Then, when Tilly was definitely sound asleep and snoring (Tilly always snored!), Mona took the rug out and worked on it some more. Over under, over under, she wove. Crisscross, crisscross, day after day was marked off on the countdown calendar.

The more she worked on the rug, the more

Mona wanted it to be fully finished before anyone saw it. She wanted it to be a surprise.

Then one morning, she was surprised herself, by a loud knock. Tilly woke up at once, and Mona scrambled to stuff the weaving under her bed. Tilly rubbed her eyes. "Huh? What's that? What are you doing, Mona?"

"I . . ."

"Mona and Tilly!" came Gilles's voice through the door. "Mr. Heartwood's called an early meeting in the kitchen. Hurry, scurry!"

Tilly raised her eyebrows, but asked no more about what Mona had been doing. Mona was relieved as they both pulled on their aprons and hurried to the kitchen.

In the kitchen, Mr. Heartwood was standing at the head of the table, with Ms. Prickles by his side. Instead of her usual smile, she wore a frown. And there was a box on the table with a label on it. BEECHNUT BISCUITS.

The box was empty.

Mona and Tilly exchanged raised-eyebrow glances, then took a seat together on the bench as others joined them. The carpenter ants, the laundry rabbits, even Tony the woodpecker, who was the hotel's security guard, were there.

What's going on? Mona wondered.

Once everyone had gathered, Mr. Heartwood cleared his throat. "Thank you all for coming. I usually wouldn't be so fussed, but because of the snow and the new guests, I must."

He took a deep breath, gazed down at the biscuit box, then looked back up at all the animals. "Some of our food is missing."

There was a collective hush, and then everyone started talking at once.

"What food?" said Maggie. "Not the carrots!"

"From where?" added Maurice. "From the kitchen?"

"From the storage room," said Ms. Prickles. "First it was the cheese, and then I noticed our chestnuts were gone. Mushrooms, too. Last night I found this box of biscuits empty. It wouldn't be so bad except we have so many guests, and the snow has delayed shipments. . . ."

"Is it a thief?" cried Tony the woodpecker. "I have been on the lookout, but sometimes it's hard to see with all this snow. . . ."

"No—it can't be," said Gilles. "Not at the Heartwood. There are *no* thieves at the Heartwood."

"There *was* a crumb I took," said one of the

carpenter ants, looking embarrassed. "Found it on the floor, yesterday. Thought no one would see that. It wasn't from the storage room, though."

"Marshal! Didn't your parents teach you not to eat off the floor?" said another ant.

"A crumb or two, no harm will do," said Mr. Heartwood. "But this is much more than that. However, there has never been a rule about taking extra food. There has never been a need. Why, we don't even have a proper door for the storage room! I am sure this is simply a case of misunderstanding. Has anyone had a midnight munch? Or perhaps a midday brunch?"

No one said anything.

Mona remembered the noise she'd heard in the storage room. But if she mentioned it, how would she explain being there herself? Tilly had believed that she was there because of the Duchess. But that wasn't the truth. Still, she hadn't been stealing food, only taking twine, twine that wasn't needed.

And she hadn't actually seen anything. Tilly leaned over, and it looked as if she was going to ask Mona something, when Mr. Heartwood continued.

"It must be a mistake with the records then," said Mr. Heartwood. "With Mrs. Higgins asleep, we can't be sure of what was and what wasn't there before."

"But I *have* checked her records," said Ms. Prickles, "and . . ."

"I know, I know, dear Ms. Prickles," sighed Mr. Heartwood. Suddenly the big badger looked very tired, and Mona remembered that he, too, was supposed to be resting like Mrs. Higgins. Instead it looked like he hadn't slept for days. "All I ask is that we please refrain from extra snacks."

Tilly's eyes were wide. She loved her snacks. "Are we really running out of food, Mr. Heartwood?"

Mr. Heartwood smiled at them reassuringly. "It's not as bad as all that. But we must be mindful.

At least until the shipment comes." He straightened the keys around his neck, and everyone waited for him to end his lecture with a rhyme. But he didn't.

It was as quiet and chilly inside the kitchen as out that morning. No one ate many seedcakes or drank much tea, Mona included.

She, like everyone else, had lost her appetite.

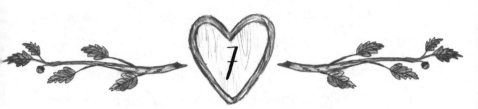

THE DEER AT THE DOOR

"Let it snow, because we'll go
To the happy Heartwood tree.
By the fire, we'll retire
And sing our melody. . . ."

Dimitry crooned, while the other members of the band accompanied him on their instruments. The Dove Tones were practicing on the stage in the ballroom late one night, while Mona swept up and Cybele listened, intrigued by the city band. Their song *was* catchy, thought Mona, even if it didn't quite ring true: not with all the wary eyes and

 67

whiskery whispers that had filled the Heartwood since the morning meeting.

A few more wintery weeks had passed, and even more food had been found missing. Everyone was upset about it. Maggie thought it was the ants. "Ants eat a lot! Way more than you think." Maurice thought it was the Duchess. "She's probably doing it just to be mean!" Tilly worried someone might think it was her. "I do eat a lot." But sometimes Mona noticed Tilly glancing at her suspiciously. Tilly had caught her twice, doing something she couldn't explain—not without giving away her secret. Why didn't she tell Tilly what she was up to? It was silly to be so stubborn, but for some reason she didn't want to tell. Not yet. That's the thing about a secret: sometimes you don't know if you're keeping it, or if it's keeping you.

She glanced across at the ballroom window. It was almost blocked by snow. Mr. Gibson had been right. Danger *was* rising, snowy danger. There was only a little sliver of moonlight at the top of the window, like a slice of cheese on a thick seedcake. But so far, the danger hadn't crept inside.

Or maybe it had. There was a thief at the Heartwood, after all. What if that thief wasn't a staff member or a guest but someone creeping in from outside?

And just as she thought that, a shadow blocked the moonlight. Only for a second though, as if something had stepped in front of the window and away again.

"Did you see that?" Mona asked Cybele.

But Cybele wasn't there. The swallow was onstage, talking with Dimitry.

Mona glanced back at the window. Probably it wasn't anything—but still. It couldn't hurt to step outside and see.

So she hurried to the back door, just down the hall. Although they'd been keeping the front door and path shoveled, they had given up on the back door, which was now blocked shut, but there was a little stepladder set up against the wall inside. Mona climbed it and slipped through a window.

Outside the Heartwood, the night was cold and quiet. The only sounds were the creaking of the trees and the soft crunch of her paws on the snow. The moon glimmered and the Heartwood windows glowed like stars.

Mona looked and listened carefully as she made her way through the courtyard. Everything was covered in white.

Suddenly, she saw something—a big silhouette—and jumped, startled. But it was just one of the snow sculptures, a bunny, half-buried now in a drift.

Mona was beginning to feel silly. Silly and cold. After all, why would anyone from outside risk traveling all the way to the hotel in this weather just to steal cheese and chestnuts, but leave the Duchess's real valuables alone? It didn't make sense.

She had decided to give up and go back inside when she saw it. A pawprint. Not just one, but a few. They were hard to make out because new snow had started to fill them, but they were definitely prints.

She began to follow them around the tree, her heart starting to race, until she almost ran headfirst into Tilly!

The squirrel was dressed in a sweater and was shouldering a shovel. Snow covered her ears, as though she'd been out in it a long time.

"Mona? What are you doing here? Don't tell me Mr. Heartwood sent you out to clean the vents, too? I told him I could do it by myself."

"Oh," said Mona. "No, he didn't. I . . ."

"He didn't? What *were* you doing, then?"

"I—I . . ." she stammered.

Tilly grumbled. "Mona, I don't like this. You keep sneaking around. What's going on?"

"I just . . . I saw something. Something from the window. I thought . . ."

Tilly's eyes narrowed.

"You saw ME," said Tilly. "Sheesh, Mona! You're acting so strange lately."

"But look! Prints in the snow. Maybe it's the thief."

Tilly rolled her eyes. "Those are MY prints! Come on, I'm finished, and I'm starving. Do you want to go roast some nuts? I always used to roast nuts for my brother, Henry. He was too little to roast them himself."

There was nothing Mona would like better than a roasted nut. But she shook her head. She needed the time to work on the rug.

"Suit yourself," said Tilly.

As they headed back to the door, Mona took another glance at the prints in the snow. Sure, some of them belonged to Tilly. But others didn't seem to. Could they belong to someone else? But who?

After that night, Mona offered to take over the task of cleaning the vents. It was hard work, and Tilly was happy not to do it, plus Mona could keep her eye out for something—anything—suspicious.

And then, one morning, she spotted something. She had just finished her task, when she froze. There, in the dim light, she could see a large shape in front of the Heartwood door—a VERY large shape!

Fear coursed through her. Was it a wolf? A fox? She couldn't quite see yet. But then, a second later, she could. It wasn't a wolf or a fox. It was a deer!

A deer would never fit inside the Heartwood! What was he doing here?

"Hello?" she called out. "Hello!"

But she was just a mouse and too far away for the deer to hear her. She had to get closer.

As she did, she could see how small he was. And also, what he was doing! He wasn't knocking on the door or waiting at it. He was eating it! Well, the wreath on it, at least.

"Hey!" cried Mona as loudly as she could. "Stop that!"

The deer's ears twitched, and he turned to face her. He had big brown eyes, and his mouth was filled with a green bough, which he dropped in surprise. He stumbled backward, his hooves slipping on the path.

"Oh!" he cried. "I didn't mean . . . I wasn't going to eat it. I mean, it looked so good, but I just was going to smell it, and then . . ."

"That's our wreath," said Mona. "You can't just eat the Heartwood wreath!"

The deer nodded. "I know. I know! I . . . was . . . just . . . hungry."

"Oh," said Mona, suddenly feeling bad. Actually, the deer *did* look thin—and young. "What are you doing here? Don't you have somewhere to go?"

The deer shook his head. "I'm a whole year old. It's my first winter alone," he said. "I was doing great. I even got my own job. I pulled the Duchess here all by myself."

"So that's how the Duchess got here," said Mona.

"Yep, it was me! I was so good, I didn't spill anything off her sleigh. She said I could pull her home when the snow melts."

"Home? But I thought she was going to a conference."

The deer blinked. "Maybe. I'm not so good at remembering. My parents told me all the places where I should go to get food, but I can't remember any of them." He sighed. "I guess, I guess I'd better go. . . ." He trailed off, as if unsure where that would be. "Unless, maybe . . . Do you need any pulling? I'm good at pulling things."

"We don't need any pulling," said Mona and could see the disappointment in the deer's eyes. "But, well . . . why don't I ask Mr. Heartwood if we can help you."

"Really?" said the deer. "You'd do that?"

"Of course," said Mona. "Just wait here. What's your name?"

The deer gave a blank look, and Mona wondered if he'd forgotten that, too, but then he said, "Francis! My name's Francis."

"I'm Mona," she said, then headed through the front door, with a smile. Francis reminded her of Brumble the bear, who was forgetful, too, except the deer was a lot smaller and thinner. But not small compared to her or Tilly. Her smile turned to a frown.

Mr. Heartwood wouldn't be happy about this. A deer was a very big mouth to feed. But when she glanced back, as she stepped through the door, she could see every one of poor Francis's ribs. And she was pretty sure that Mr. Heartwood wouldn't be happy about *that* either.

No one, after all, had a bigger heart than Mr. Heartwood.

THE SPOTTED SLEEPWALKERS

The Heartwood lobby was quiet except for the crackling of the fire that lit the room. On the front desk stood a sign: RING FOR SERVICE. Behind the desk, Mr. Heartwood's door was slightly ajar and light spilled out.

"Mr. Heartwood?" Mona said softly, pushing the door open a little more.

He was there . . . but he wasn't working. He was snoring.

The badger's big head was on his wooden desk, one paw on top of a letter. Although the letter was facedown, Mona could still read the stamp:

She took a hesitant step forward, filled with curiosity.

"Ack, no, no! Jay, don't go," Mr. Heartwood mumbled. "That can't be your news. . . . How on earth could they ever lose . . . ?" He snorted and thumped his paw on the letter. Mona took a startled step backward.

She was considering fetching Gilles when Mr. Heartwood sat up, jolting awake of his own accord.

"Miss Mona the mouse, maid of the house!" he said. "What brings you here at this early hour?"

"Oh, I'm so sorry to disturb you, Mr. Heartwood," she said. "I can go."

"Not at all," said the badger. "It's a difficult thing, to shake off the sleep that hibernation time brings. I was expecting much more time for napping, but, well . . . as you know, we have more guests than we can count." He consulted a ledger on his desk. "Twenty-four ants, four doves, seven rabbits, including the Duchess. It's a good thing she didn't bring any of her staff along with her."

"Actually, Mr. Heartwood, that's why I'm here." Mona explained about Francis. When she was done, Mr. Heartwood gave a mighty sigh.

"I could tell him to go," said Mona. "I didn't promise anything. I didn't know what to do."

"No, no," said Mr. Heartwood, "he may stay. Though because of his size, he must shelter outside."

He sighed again, and glanced up at the striped hat that hung from a hook on a wall—the one he'd worn as St. Slumber. "To think already two months have passed since the St. Slumber Supper. I could use another night of celebration like that. Free of care and unaware . . ."

Unaware of what, Mona wasn't sure, but a party sounded good. She replied "Me too," and she smiled thinking about finally finishing the rug and presenting it to him. That would be like a mini St. Slumber's celebration—and she was sure it would cheer him up. Only a little more and it would be done. She couldn't wait until that night, when Tilly would be asleep and she could get to work.

But Tilly, it seemed, would *never* fall asleep. Mona's friend was fuming about Francis. "Seriously, Mona! Another guest!" she groaned from her bed. "I can't believe Mr. Heartwood said we'd feed him!"

"But he's really sweet," said Mona.

"Do you know how much deer eat? Like, five seedcakes in one gobble." She sighed. "It's a good thing I like you," she muttered. Finally her friend stopped tossing and turning. And, a moment later, started to snore.

The moment she did, Mona got up very, very quietly. She knelt down and pulled the rug out from underneath her bed. It was getting so big, she had to fold it in two for it to fit. The twine, most of it made from thin strips of pounded bark, was surprisingly soft, and sunshiny gold. *Maybe it will remind everyone of the sunny days coming,* thought Mona. She was really proud of it.

She reached back under her bed for more twine but couldn't feel any. Was she out again? She had used up so much! All the twine from the gift-giving, and all the spare twine she could find in the garden shed, too. She'd even scavenged a few scraps from the kitchen. She'd have to try the storage room again. Maybe there was some twine tucked away at the back that she'd missed. If she hurried, she might even be able to finish the rug tonight!

Carefully, she folded the rug in two again and tucked it back under her bed. The bedroom door creaked as she opened it, but Tilly didn't stir. Mona shut it behind her as softly as a sigh.

Everyone was in their rooms now. Even the kitchen was dark. But still she tiptoed. She didn't want to wake anyone. When she reached the hibernation hall, however—the one place where everyone really should be in bed—she was startled to find someone up.

Two someones, actually!

Two small spotted shapes were slowly crawling down the hall in the dim lantern light.

Then she saw a third, staring up at the lantern hanging from the wall, his antennae slowly twitching back and forth like the hands of a clock.

"Mr. Dotson, is that you?" said Mona, recognizing his particular nightcap, which was red with black polka dots, just like his body.

But Mr. Dotson didn't reply. He just gazed at her dreamily. He wasn't really awake at all. He was sleepwalking. Mona gently directed him back to his room, along with the other two, Mrs. Dotson and their daughter, Dotty.

Luckily, the rest of the ladybugs were sleeping in their suite, shifting back and forth only slightly in their little beds. After settling the three back under their blankets, Mona crept out of their room, wondering what had roused them.

There were still a few weeks left on the calendar until hibernation time was over. Probably more, with it being so cold outside. Of course, it wasn't as cold deep down here. Actually, it wasn't cold at all. . . .

Mona gulped. *The vents must be blocked again!* The snow WAS falling fast. . . .

Forget the twine! Mona hurried back down the hall. As she passed the storage room, she felt cool air coming from its doorway.

That was strange. If some of the vents were blocked, shouldn't they *all* be? Unless . . . unless her earlier suspicions—the ones she'd dismissed as silly—were true: a thief was sneaking into the Heartwood from outside!

A thief with claws that *scritch-scratched* at night and left pawprints in the snow.

And if the vent in the storage room was cleared right now, that could only mean one of two things! Either the thief had just left—or he was still there right now!

Mona froze, fear bristling up and down her fur. What should she do? If the thief *was* still there, could she catch him? Was she brave enough?

She listened, to see if she could tell if the thief was still inside, when there was a voice behind her.

"What are you doing here, Mona?"

It was Tilly, standing behind her.

"*Shhh,*" said Mona quickly.

"What's going on?"

Mona hushed her again. "Tilly, it's the thief," said Mona, in a whisper. "I think the thief's in the storage room. . . ."

Tilly crossed her arms. "A likely story."

"It's the truth!" said Mona.

"I don't think so. I think you're lying to me."

"I'm not!"

"What are you doing down here in the first place, then?"

"I—I . . . can't explain that right now," stammered Mona. "There's no time."

But Tilly didn't stop, "You haven't had any time for me lately. We didn't go skating or roast nuts. What *are* you up to, Mona?"

"Nothing!" said Mona, feeling her cheeks flush. "Well . . ."

"Don't tell me, then. I thought we were friends. Friends share everything. You've been sneaking around with all sorts of secrets. I'm not friends with a sneak."

"I'm not a sneak!" cried Mona. "I'm only sneaking around because of YOU!"

"ME?!" exclaimed Tilly. "What do you mean, ME?! Are you saying that I am the thief?!"

"No! That's not what I meant!

I . . ." But now Mona wasn't sure what she meant.
After all, Tilly had been sneaking around all the
time, too. And she did eat a lot! Mona was bristling
with anger and confusion when . . .

THUMP!

A loud noise stopped them both. And it was
coming from the storage room!

The Shadow in the Storage Room

Mona and Tilly stared at each other, wide-eyed. Tilly's tail bristled.

"I *told* you," whispered Mona.

"*Shhh!*" said Tilly.

They waited, but the sound did not come again, so Tilly scampered to the storage room, Mona behind her. They pushed aside the curtain, entering just in time to see a shadow at the back of the room flit between two rows of food.

"Hey! Stop!" shouted Tilly.

But the thief didn't. Instead, it—for Mona couldn't make out whether it was a he or she, or even what kind of animal it was—turned, ran, and leapt right into the wall.

Right into the vent.

"Oh no you don't!" cried Tilly, speeding down the aisle, almost tripping over a spilled box of nuts, obviously the cause of the thump. Mona chased after her.

When Tilly scrambled into the vent, Mona did, too. The tunnel was dark and musty. Tilly only just fit, and Mona got a faceful of fur. Still, Tilly moved forward, fast, worming her way up, up, up.

Mona couldn't get a glimpse of the thief through Tilly's giant tail. What kind of animal was it? What kind of animal stole? Not a good one, that was certain. Should they really chase after it? Shouldn't they tell Mr. Heartwood? Shouldn't they get help? She should tell Tilly to stop. But it was too late.

Tilly had reached the knothole at the top of the vent and dove out onto the snow, setting off after

91

the creature who was speeding away across the sea of white.

A blast of cold shook Mona from head to tail, but she jumped out, too, and rushed forth. The thief was in the distance, a large dark shape, and Mona still couldn't make out what or who it was.

Mona raced after Tilly and the thief, through the courtyard (which wasn't actually a courtyard anymore; the blackberry walls were completely buried by snow), past the bushes where Francis was sleeping (she could just see his nose peeking out), and into Fernwood Forest.

Although Mona ran as fast as she could, she quickly fell farther and farther behind. She was

just a mouse, after all. Would she lose sight of them altogether?

Mona had never been this deep into the forest before, never been farther than the Heartwood. She had no idea what she might find.

Now, in the silvery light of the moon, she was discovering—pools of frozen water, giant trees, and bushes covered in ice and snow, but not just that: a wreath woven from thin twigs, hanging from a bush. A chimney sticking out of a snow-buried stump. A doorknob poking from the side of a tree, near a large branch. Small hints here and there of other animals hidden away.

But there were fewer and fewer signs as the thief

plunged down a snowy bank and sped over an icy part of the stream, Tilly right behind it.

Mona slipped and slid but didn't fall. There is a certain balance that comes when a small animal's heart pounds, a certain phenomenal strength and speed—and how Mona's heart pounded! Not from fear so much as anger, anger at this thief, and even at Tilly.

It was just like Tilly to leap into something without really thinking about it! If they got into big trouble, it would be all Tilly's fault. At least now Tilly could see it wasn't HER who was stealing food. That she wasn't lying. But those things wouldn't really matter if they were both attacked by the thief or lost in the snow!

Fear outweighed anger when all at once the thief disappeared into a large snowbank. Where had the thief gone?

Not long after, Mona understood. The mound

of snow was actually a giant buried log, the top edge just peeking out from a heavy layer of white. It was the thief's lair!

"Stop!" Mona cried out to Tilly.

But it was too late. Tilly dove in after it.

And Mona followed. She plunged into the hole in the snow and into darkness, landing with a *thud*.

She blinked and took a few cautious steps as her eyes adjusted.

There in front of her lay Tilly, splayed on the dirt floor of the log. Towering over her was none other than the thief!

A rat!

Mona had seen rats before, but never any as fearsome as this. His tail was scarred, and one ear was ripped in two. His fur was matted from the snow, and through it she could see his bones. He was thin like Francis, but unlike Francis, he didn't look frail. His sinewy muscles were all flexed. Even his tail was flexed, and his teeth, long and white and sharp, were bared.

Tilly was trembling.

"Now you've done it!" the rat said in a raspy voice.

Mona swallowed a squeak and scoured the floor, and—much to her surprise—found just what she needed. A small, sharp twig. She grabbed it and pointed it shakily at the rat. She was trying to summon her courage to use it if he lunged, when a tiny piping voice shouted:

"Please! Don't hurt Hood!"

10

HOOD'S HOME

Mona glanced around, her eyes adjusting even more to the darkness. She gasped. Surrounding her were animals—young animals, only a few seasons old. There were three raccoons huddled together, sucking their claws, and a roly-poly porcupine with a bandage on her paw, as though perhaps she'd pricked herself with her own quills.

Two little rabbits were sitting near the log's entrance. One was clutching a toy—a whittled wooden carrot. And now Mona saw that's what she was holding in her paw,

not a stick, but another wooden carrot! Beside the rabbits stood a red squirrel, half the size of Tilly, with a bushy tail that was bigger than his body.

"Please, don't hurt Hood," he said again.

"Hood?" said Mona, dropping the wooden carrot back on the ground.

"That'd be me." The rat turned to face her, and she was surprised again. His hunched back and grizzled fur had led her to believe he was old, but his face was young, though he was missing half his whiskers.

The little squirrel ran over to him, and the other animals soon joined them.

"Are you okay, Hood? Are you? Are you?" came a chorus of tiny voices.

"I'm fine," said the rat, his gaze shifting between Mona and Tilly, who was slowly getting up. "It was . . . a misunderstanding."

The little animals seemed to relax, and quickly

gathered around Mona and Tilly, bombarding them with questions.

"Who are you?"

"Mona," she replied. "I'm a maid at the—"

"Why are you here?"

"I was following—"

"Are you a friend of Hood's?"

"Do you want to see our house?"

"Yes, show them our house, Hood!" replied one of the rabbits, and the others agreed. "Show them! Show them!" they chanted.

Reluctantly, the rat clambered up on a chair and lit a lantern above them. He waved a paw around the log. "Welcome to Hood's Home for Orphaned Animals."

Now Mona could see that it *was* a home . . . the strangest home she had ever seen. Everything was sideways!

On the wall opposite her was what once must

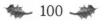

have been a beautiful fireplace, but it was completely on its side. Instead of housing flames, it held blankets and some toys. A bookshelf lay beside it, with all the shelves running up and down rather than left to right.

On the ceiling was a door! Hanging from the doorknob was the light that the rat had lit. And to Mona's left, once a ceiling, was a wall with a hole in it, from which another small animal peered: a little mole.

This had clearly once been a beautiful home— grand like the Heartwood. But it had fallen over long ago.

Instead of the smell of buttery seedcakes or roasted nuts, the only smell here was a faintly rotting one, and instead of the sounds of a crackling fire and song, there was only the creaking of the ceiling, groaning under the weight of the newly fallen snow.

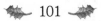

Despite these differences, one thing was very similar to the hotel. Above the fireplace, a sign hung from the wall, sideways though, and Mona tilted her head to read it.

WE LIVE WITH LOVE AND LAUGHTER,

NOT WITH SNARLS OR GROWLS.

It reminded Mona of the sign that hung in the Heartwood lobby. Mona was filled with questions and was about to ask some of them when the little red squirrel pointed to the sign.

"See! You can't hurt Hood. It's a *rule*. You know. No biting or fighting. No pinching or pricking. Not *even* if you have quills."

At this he looked over at the porcupine, who replied, huffily, "I *know*, Henry. I never MEAN to prick you."

"Really?" Henry humphed.

Before he could say anything else, Tilly cried, "Henry?" She pushed past Hood. "Henry, is that *you*?"

The little red squirrel's tail bristled out wide, just like Tilly's always did when she was excited.

"Tilly!" he cried.

"I knew it! I knew it, I knew it, I knew it!" The little squirrel dashed into Tilly's outstretched arms. They fell over onto the floor, but they didn't care. They were laughing and hugging and rolling around while Mona and the others watched in amazement.

"Now, that just takes the cheese, doesn't it?" Hood said, gruffly.

"What takes the cheese?" asked the mole. "What does, Hood?"

"Henry's found his sister," replied the rat.

"I *told* you I'd find her!" exclaimed Henry, who was still clinging to Tilly's side.

"I found *you*, you nutcase!" Tilly said back, rubbing the fur on his head till it stood on end.

Mona felt a pang of wishing and wondering. She couldn't remember anything about her family. But then she thought of the smell of seedcakes and soft whiskers kissing her good night. Well, maybe she could remember a little.

Her thoughts were interrupted by Hood, who said, "Who'd've thought Henry's sister was there, right at the Heartwood, where I've been every night."

"So you ARE the thief! My brother's been staying with a *thief*?!" said Tilly.

"Hood's not a thief. Honest, Till. He saw the coyotes chasing me and led them away. He brought me here. Hood's a hero. He saved me!"

Tilly was taken aback, and turned to the rat. "You did?"

Hood shrugged. "Coyotes are bad. The wild is worse." He brushed his paw to his missing whiskers.

"Well. I still want you to explain," said Tilly, crossing her arms.

Mona wanted to know, too.

"I've only ever taken what wasn't really needed," said Hood slowly.

"'Cause you were like us, right, Hood?" said the porcupine. "You were an orphan, too."

"Tell the story!" said one rabbit.

"Tell it, Hood," said the other.

Hood nodded. "Maybe that's easiest." He straightened up and closed his eyes. "It was a long time ago now, during a hot summer. There was a fire. . . ."

"A fire like a wolf," interrupted Henry. "Worse! 'Cause it ate animals AND trees. It was the scariest thing ever. But Hood knew what to do. He ran from his home toward the stream. The fire chased after him, but Hood and his family got away."

"Not my parents," said Hood. "My brothers and sisters and I were orphaned. So were many others." Hood closed his eyes.

"But it was okay," said Henry. "'Cause Hood gave them a home. Well, at first it was hard to find a good one. He searched all over the place."

Mona couldn't help but remember her own search, one that had eventually led her to the

Heartwood. If she had found Hood and his group, would she have stayed with them? Her life could have been very different. . . .

Henry continued. "Then, one day, Hood was walking along a log, and WHOOMP! He fell into it! Right through the ceiling." The little squirrel pointed with a paw up to a spot that was patched up with bark and now sagged under the weight of the snow. "Through THIS ceiling. And he was SO surprised, because he had landed in a big old fancy house that had fallen over. It was perfect." The

patch in the ceiling groaned. "Well, mostly per-fect," said Henry. "And safe from fires and wolves and coyotes. . . ."

"And completely out of food," said Hood. "Usually I can scrounge some, but the snow makes it impossible. . . ."

As though the weather were listening, the wind wailed through the hole they had used to get into the log. All the animals tensed, Mona included.

Hood gestured around him. "I figured if one grand home could shelter us, another could feed us. The Heartwood wouldn't miss a little food."

"You're wrong. We did miss the food," said Mona. "This winter has been hard for us, too."

"Hard?" said Hood. The tree groaned again. "I shouldn't have stolen, that's true, but perhaps you and I have different ideas of hard."

Mona gulped as she looked around at the faces of the little animals. Hood was right. She hadn't been hungry for a long time. She had a cozy bed to sleep in. She had a crackling fireplace to warm herself by. She had even celebrated St. Slumber's Supper.

None of these animals had, that was certain. There were no gifts of crumble or fancy aprons here. These animals needed the Heartwood and all that it offered: warm beds and a crackling fire, buttery seedcakes, and Mr. Heartwood dressed up in his pajamas. Kind, generous Mr. Heartwood. Sure, he was worried about food, but there was the shipment coming, and he wouldn't want these animals here alone and hungry, would he? Mona took a big breath.

"You didn't need to steal. You could have just knocked."

"Really?" said one of the little moles.

"Can we just knock? I want to knock!" cried another.

"My momma used to say there was a whole *room* of games at the Heartwood."

"And a whole room of honey to swim in, too!"

"Not a room," said Mona. "But honey does *always* flow at the Heartwood."

The orphans' eyes went wide with wonder.

"But don't you need farthings to stay there?" piped the little mole.

"You do," said Hood, shaking his head. "We can't go."

"This is different," said Tilly, glancing at Henry. "This is an emergency. Mona's right."

Mona smiled. At least Tilly agreed with her.

"I don't know," said Hood. "I'm not looking for charity. I would rather manage on our own here. I wouldn't know how to explain . . ."

"Don't worry," said Mona. "I can explain for you. We just need to get to the Heartwood. Everything will be fine. I promise."

Creeeeeeak. The log groaned again.

After a long pause, Hood nodded. "I guess we don't have much choice."

All the orphans cheered. Some even jumped up

and hugged Mona tight. Tilly, too, and Tilly and Mona exchanged a hesitant smile. They hadn't spoken, not really, since the fight. *I'll explain everything when we get back,* thought Mona. *No more secrets.*

Everything *was* going to work out fine, she thought.

The log, however, continued to creak and groan above them, as if it had its doubts.

THE MIDNIGHT MUNCH

The walk back to the Heartwood was long and cold. The snow swirled around them, thicker now, whipped about by the wind. It was dark, darker than before, even though it would be morning soon. Any trace of the moon was blocked by the falling flakes. Hood and Mona led the way, while Tilly and Henry took up the rear, obviously sharing stories, though now was not really the time. Hood urged them all to hurry, and to stay together. The thicker the snow fell, the harder it was to see.

As they passed a large snowbank, the mole, who was walking with Mona, said, "I smell something!

Seeds and nuts and cheese. Is it the Heartwood?"

"Not yet," Mona said, squeezing his paw. "You're just imagining it."

"Nuh-uh! I bet Henry smells it, too! He's got the best nose!"

"You can ask Henry once we reach the Heartwood, Matthew," said Hood. "No time to stop now."

Mona smiled and glanced back, but she couldn't see Henry or Tilly. The snow was falling too thick, too fast. She was glad they had left Hood's Home when they did. She hoped the Heartwood was close. For a moment, Mona thought she smelled something, too. Now SHE was imagining things.

Her stomach began to rumble. When had *she* last eaten something? Not for a while, and she dreamed, as you do when you are hungry, of her favorite meal—a big buttery seedcake and a mug of hot honey.

It was early morning when they finally arrived at the Heartwood, but no one could stop the excitement of the orphans, who after expressing their delight over the secret heart-shaped lock that opened the front door, burst into the lobby in a flurry of snow and shouts.

"A fireplace!" cried one of the rabbits, staring at it. "A real fireplace. And it's right-side up."

"And LOOK. There IS a staircase, straight up to the stars!" cried the other.

"It's SO big!"

"And SO beautiful!"

They began jumping on and climbing over everything immediately. But Hood looked wary and stood near the door.

Mona remembered feeling apprehensive herself when she had first entered the Heartwood so many months ago. It seemed like all the orphans were accounted for, except for Henry. She was just waiting for him and Tilly to come in when there was a

voice: "Now, now, what can this be? What guests arrive at quarter to three?"

Mr. Heartwood strode from the hallway into the lobby. He was wearing his nightcap, but his keys still hung around his neck.

Was he up working? Mona wondered. But it was so late. Actually, early!

The orphans froze at the sight of the big badger. Mona was about to explain when there was another voice.

"Indeed. What is going on here? How dare you disturb my slumber? Rest at the Heartwood—*humph*."

Standing at the top of the staircase was none other than the Duchess, wearing a long night-gown and wielding her eye mask like a scepter. The Duchess sniffed and surveyed the scene in the lobby. "And what ragtag group is this?"

The orphans, gathering together, gazed up at her in amazement.

"We're no ragtag group," said Hood, stepping into the lobby at last. "We're from an orphanage. Hood's Home for Orphaned Animals. And I'm Hood."

Mr. Heartwood's eyebrows rose.

"I invited them here," said Mona. "They need food. They were the ones who were taking, well . . ."

Mr. Heartwood's eyebrows rose higher.

"Not ones—just me," said Hood. "I was planning to repay you for everything come spring."

"Repay what?" shrieked the Duchess. "What IS going on?"

Mr. Heartwood looked very grave. He was shaking his head. But instead of saying anything to Hood, he turned to Mona.

"Miss Mouse, is this true? Is their coming due to you?"

Mona nodded proudly. "I knew you wouldn't mind, Mr. Heartwood, that you'd see they're really hungry. And they weren't safe. I couldn't leave them in their house. It was going to collapse."

But then, all at once, she could tell something was terribly wrong. Instead of smiling and agreeing, Mr. Heartwood shook his head and gave Mona a stern look.

"Oh Miss Mouse, tonight of all nights. But of course, how were you to . . . ?"

"What do you mean?" said Mona. "What's going on, Mr. Heartwood?"

"I demand to know, myself," said the Duchess. "At once!"

"Yes, of course. Miss Hazeline, please head to the ballroom, where all will be explained to you. I was gathering everyone there, the staff, as well as the hibernators."

The Duchess crossed her arms and strode toward the hall, but Mona's ears were buzzing.

"What do you mean, about the hibernators?" she whispered, almost afraid to ask.

"They're up," said Mr. Heartwood. "They're up, and they've eaten everything."

They *were* up.

The ballroom was full of the hibernators, half-awake, in their nightclothes, and covered in crumbs. Mr. and Mrs. Dotson and Dotty, as well as the rest of the ladybugs, were spread out across a table, like a black-and-red spotted tablecloth. The toads, rubbing red-rimmed eyes, were sitting with the chipmunks, who looked like they hadn't just eaten honey but had bathed in it, and no amount of nettle-stem napkins provided by the laundry rabbits could help clean them up. The smallest chipmunk was the biggest mess.

Not only was he sticky, he had a terrible case of bed-fur. Mr. Gibson, the groundhog, was searching the room and muttering, "No shadow. No shadow in sight. Must be still sleeping, sensible thing . . ." while the turtles trundled after him,

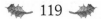

confused, asking, "Is it shadow-spotting time? So soon?" Even the hedgehogs, Mr. and Mrs. Higgins, were up, looking extremely befuddled.

"What is going on?" Mona overheard Mrs. Higgins ask Ms. Prickles. "Why did no one wake me to warn me of the problems . . . ?"

"You *were* awake, Mrs. Higgins," replied the porcupine. "You were awake and eating all my roasted acorns. It was the heat, you see. . . ."

So it was the vents! Mona knew the snow had been blocking them. She should have told someone, but then

she heard Hood, and there was no chance. Tilly had come and, well . . . Where was Tilly? Mona glanced around, but didn't see her. Instead, she noticed Hood and his orphans clustered at the back of the room, looking out of place. Hood had offered to repay Mr. Heartwood for the food in the spring—but that wouldn't help right now, if the hibernators had eaten all the food! But surely there was *some* left.

Her thoughts were interrupted by Mr. Heartwood's booming voice.

"Staff and guests, my apologies to all." His voice resounded in the room, as he stood on the stage. "But I am here with grave news." He took a deep breath. "The Heartwood Hotel has run out of food."

"No food!" shrieked Duchess Hazeline. "It cannot be!"

"No honeyed carrots?" said Maurice the laundry rabbit.

"There were honeyed carrots?" repeated the little rabbits.

"This must be a joke!" cried one of the doves.

"I know a joke," said Matthew. "It's Henry's favorite. Henry, Henry?" The little mole squinted his eyes.

"Hush," said Hood. "This isn't the time for jokes. We need to fix what we've done. . . ."

"No, no. It's *our* fault," said Mr. Dotson from the tabletop. "If only we hadn't woken. . . ."

"Don't blame yourselves. It was the—" started Ms. Prickles.

"That snow! It's to blame! It just keeps falling and falling," said one of the ants.

"Enough," commanded Mr. Heartwood. "No more pointing paws—or antennae. We can't work with what-ifs. We must work with what is. And that means staying here at the Heartwood and sharing what little we have left. We can melt snow

for warm drinks, and make do with the few stores in the kitchen and in the rooms."

"Until the shipment comes, of course. Right, Mr. Heartwood?" said Gilles.

"I am afraid that is the other news I must share with you all," said the badger. "I received a letter a few days ago. Our shipment was stuck in a snowbank. When the squirrels tried to move it, the sleigh broke. They had no choice but to abandon it. I have no clue where it is, and even if I knew, we could not go out and fetch it. I did not act upon the news before now, as I hoped that our food would last until the snow ceased and we could safely search for the shipment. But the snow has not stopped, and our food has run out. I wish I could give you better news. But I cannot give what I do not have."

Mona gulped and glanced over at the orphans. She'd done just that, promising them food and shelter. Now what? What would they do? What would

they *all* do? Her stomach twisted with knots.

The Duchess had an answer. "I shall depart at once!" she cried. "I should never have left my burrow in the first place. Some Heartwood."

"And we Dove Tones can return to the city," said Dimitry. "There is always food to be scavenged there."

"We will leave, too," added Hood. "But—"

"I don't want to," said one rabbit.

"Me neither," said the other, and burst into tears. Soon all the orphans were crying. Everyone was yelling now, and Mona's ears hurt.

"You can't leave!" said Mr. Heartwood, instantly silencing them all. "No one must leave in this snow, I insist. It is too dangerous. Together we will find a way with the little we have."

For a moment, Hood looked convinced. But then a second later, he replied in a louder voice. "I must leave."

"Unexpected as you were . . . I—" replied Mr. Heartwood.

"I *must* leave," interrupted Hood. "I have to!"

"There, there, dearie," said Ms. Prickles. "We forgive you. It'll be all right. It's surprising what I can do with a salty stone and some water."

But Mona could tell by looking at Hood that it wasn't all right. He was completely frantic, scanning the room, his tail twitching, his paws shaking.

Before he could say what the matter was, Mona knew, and her paws and tail began to shake, too.

It was Henry. Henry was missing. And so was Tilly.

"They're still out there!" cried Hood.

"Who is?" demanded Mr. Heartwood.

"Tilly!" Mona choked. "It's Tilly, Mr. Heartwood. Tilly and her brother."

THE GREATEST GIFT

All the other problems, big as they might be, suddenly seemed small. After all, most animals knew how to go days without food. They could survive almost anything—as long as they were safe and together, warm and hidden from the wicked wild. But Tilly and Henry were stuck in the snowstorm.

Mr. Heartwood's eyes went wide. His nostrils flared. "It can't be."

But it was.

Tilly and Henry had been at the end of the line. And they had never made it back to the Heartwood. Mona's heart raced.

"We have to rescue them!" cried Mona. "Tilly's my friend."

"I'll go," said Hood.

"Me too! Me too!" said the little mole. "Henry's *my* friend!"

"If we all bundle up—" started Ms. Prickles.

"I have plenty of knits—" said Mrs. Higgins.

"We'll leave at once—" said Gilles.

"You will be lost, too!" growled Mr. Heartwood. "In snow like this, there is no way."

"There has to be!" said Hood.

"What about the lights? Surely you can see the lights of the Heartwood from a distance," said Cybele.

"Or hear it, perhaps?" said Dimitry. "We can play our instruments loudly, and you can hear your way back."

"The wind whistles stronger than any voice," said Mr. Heartwood. "And the snow shrouds everything from sight."

"I know!" squeaked Matthew. "We can all hold paws and claws and tails, and make a big chain, so we never really leave the Heartwood at all!"

"Paws and claws and tails would never do," said Mr. Heartwood. "But . . ." He paused, his bushy eyebrows raised. "Twine would work. Only we have none long enough. However, if all our twine was knotted together . . . But that would take nights of work."

Nights of work. Twine knotted together. Mona's heart thumped. "I have some!" she burst.

"Miss Mouse, what do you mean?" asked Mr. Heartwood.

"I've been working on something, something for the Heartwood," she explained quickly. "But it doesn't matter now. . . . I mean, what matters is that I have some twine—lots of it—all tied together."

And she did. She had the rug.

It was too big and heavy for her to carry upstairs

alone, so she whispered in Ms. Prickles's ear, and together they set off to get it. When they unrolled it on the ballroom floor, larger and prettier than Mona could have imagined, everyone gasped.

"My word!" said Gilles.

"You did this all by yourself?" said Mrs. Higgins.

Mona nodded, glancing at Mr. Heartwood. Mr. Heartwood didn't say anything. He had placed one paw over his heart. It was the best reaction of all. But she didn't hesitate. She bent down and began to undo it.

"Are you sure . . . ?" started Ms. Prickles.

"I'm sure," said Mona.

Nights and mornings of work quickly disappeared as Mona undid her gift, and Mrs. Higgins carefully rolled the twine into a ball behind her. Everyone wanted to go, but Mr. Heartwood insisted the fewer that risked themselves the better. Of course, that didn't apply to him—and he declared he'd lead the way.

"No," said Mona. "You have to stay here with the hotel. I'll go."

"We'll go together," replied Hood. "I know the way back to my home."

And so it was decided. Everyone else pitched in to help them prepare, offering mittens and scarves, lights and a few meager snacks.

There was only one animal who stood off in the corner, her nose in the air. It was, of course, the Duchess.

Everyone else was working together now, and Mona's heart was full of hope.

At last, when the rug was completely unraveled—and Mona and Hood bundled warmly, with some supplies, including warm blankets, packed on their backs—they set out. They clutched one end of the twine in their mittened paws, and the other end was tied securely to the Heartwood Hotel.

THE STUCK SHIPMENT

Immediately, Mona's hope faltered. The blizzard was a beast now—a beast as bad as a wolf, or worse! It bit at her ears and her nose, clawed at her fur, and pulled at her tail. It howled in her ears and hurt her head. The mittens provided by Ms. Prickles didn't do much good. Her paws were numb and barely able to keep the twine clutched tight.

They had only gone a few steps, and already

the Heartwood, that massive tree, was hidden from view by the snow.

Still, Hood pushed on ahead, the twine swaying between him and Mona. "Follow me," he cried over the wind.

That was the plan—head back toward Hood's Home and try to find Tilly and Henry along the way.

"Tilly!" Mona shouted.

"Save your voice," Hood shouted back. "She won't . . ."

Even Hood's own words were snatched by the wailing wind. So Mona stopped shouting, though it was hard. She wanted to cry out for Tilly, wanted to reach with voice and paw and even whiskers if she had to, to find her friend. The longer they

trekked, the more her paws ached—and her heart, too. It was easy to imagine losing their way now, in this blinding snow, and Mona clutched the twine tighter. At least it kept them together, and tethered back home to the Heartwood. She gave it a tug. It seemed strangely slack.

"Hood! Stop!" cried Mona. "Something's wrong."

But the wind howled and Hood cried back, "No time for a song!"

"No . . . something's WRONG!" shouted Mona, but Hood just kept trudging ahead. Mona gave the twine another gentle tug. It was definitely looser. What if it was one of her knots that had come undone? Or maybe the twine had snagged on something and snapped?

She didn't have a chance to call out again, because she tripped on something buried in the snow. She caught herself just in time.

What had she tripped over? A branch? A trap?

A second later, she saw. It was something thin and colorful. The twine! How long had they been circling back on themselves?

"Look!" cried Mona.

This time Hood heard and turned.

"We're going in circles!"

"We can't give up!" said Hood. Mona agreed. But then he added, "I know where we're going!" and she was doubtful.

But before they had any chance to argue, Hood spun around and plowed forward again. The twine went taut, and Mona was very nearly swept off her paws.

There was no arguing with him, especially now that they could barely hear each other again.

Hood was just as stubborn as Tilly.

When Mona had started working at the Heartwood, Tilly had been so difficult, Mona had thought the squirrel hated her. She had almost left the Heartwood for good because of it. But then she

discovered that Tilly had lost her family and was worried Mona might take her job. Tilly couldn't bear to lose anything else. She had been afraid.

Mona was afraid now.

She and Tilly had never even made up from their fight. Tilly had called her a sneak. And she had said that it was Tilly's fault. But it wasn't. Mona should have told Tilly what she was doing. That's what friends did. They shared things. Were those really the last things they would say to each other?

Mona clung to her twine. All those nights worrying about a gift and working on the rug. It seemed so important.

But it wasn't really.

Friends were important. Friends and food and the Heartwood. Those were the biggest gifts. Not anything wrapped and tied in twine.

Tears pricked at her eyes.

She sniffed and sniffed, trying not to cry. And

then she sniffed . . . and she smelled something. Seedcakes? She sniffed again. Yes, it definitely was!

"Seedcakes!" she shouted over the wind.

"No breaks!" Hood shouted back.

"NO! *Seedcakes*, Hood!"

And it wasn't just seedcakes. Mona could smell other things now, too: acorns and cheese and licorice.

Was she just imagining it?

And then suddenly she stopped.

That was exactly what she had said to the little mole not so long ago, on their way back from the Heartwood! She had thought the food was imaginary, but maybe it wasn't. Maybe it was . . . "The shipment!" she cried. The little mole had said Henry had a great sense of smell.

If Henry had smelled food, Tilly would have insisted on checking it out. And if they had found the shipment, well . . . maybe that's how they got lost. And maybe that's where Mona would find them, too.

Yes, she knew it, from her whiskers to her heart to her nose.

The twine jolted in her paws. "Mona," said Hood, "I said no stopping!" His face was fierce, and twitched where his whiskers would have been. But only for a moment. Because then . . . he must have smelled it, too, for his eyes went wide, and he pointed his nose to the sky and began to sniff. Mona joined him.

Sniff, sniff, sniff. They followed their noses through the white, between two trees, and toward a large mound of snow. . . .

To the Rescue!

It looked just like a large snowbank, but it wasn't. The wind had blown some of the snow away, and Mona could see crates and bags, stamped with the black acorn mark of the Squirrels' Delivery Service. One crate was cracked in two, and from it came the smell of seedcakes.

It was the shipment! It had to be! One of the sleigh's runners was splintered. Mr. Heartwood had said the sleigh had broken.

But there was more than just the smell, there was a sound, too, the faint sound of singing carried by the wind.

"This is the way we brush our tails,
Brush our tails, brush our tails.
This is the way we brush our tails,
Early in the morning. . . ."

"Come on, Henry, there's got to be a better song than that."

Mona recognized the voice at once. "TILLY!"

"Mona? MONA!" the voice came piping back.

And then, from a hollow in the snow right in front of them, under the shipment, poked a head— the whiskery red-furred face of none other than Mona's best friend. Tilly scrambled out of the snow, and a moment later, Henry emerged, too.

"I knew they would come! I knew it!" he cried.

"Henry!" Hood exclaimed. "We found you!"

Henry and Hood leapt into each other's arms, and Tilly and Mona did, too, and then there was a flurry of excitement and hugging and cries of delight.

Once everyone had settled down, and Hood had wrapped Henry and Tilly in the blankets they had brought, they shared a small box of treats that Henry had dug out from one of the crates. The box was full of candied bark, maple-dipped moss, acorn macaroons, and even cheese. It was just what they needed to give them the energy to return home. Never had cheese tasted so good, and Mona could feel her whiskers relax.

"It was my nose that found the food," said Henry. "Can we bring it back, Hood? Can we?"

"I keep trying to tell him we can't," Tilly said to Mona. "Taking a treat or two won't hurt, but we can't take more. Not when it doesn't belong to us."

"It does!" said Mona. "Our shipment was stuck—and Mr. Heartwood said the sleigh was broken. This must be it."

"Our food was stuck?!" Tilly groaned. "No *wonder* Mr. Heartwood has been extra stressed. You can always tell. He doesn't rhyme."

"So we *can* bring it back? We can have beech-nut biscuits? With butter?" cried Henry.

"Later, when the snow stops," said Hood. "We need to bring you back first. Let's tie the twine. . . ."

"Twine?" asked Tilly. "What twine?"

"From my rug," said Mona.

"What rug?"

"That was my secret," said Mona. "I was making a rug—it was for you and everyone at the Heartwood. To replace the one the Duchess ruined.

I've been working on it all this time. I wanted to give everyone a gift."

"Oh," said Tilly. For once the squirrel looked at a loss for what to say. "That explains . . . That's really nice but . . . but you didn't have to. . . ."

"Actually it's a good thing she did," said Hood. "That twine kept Mona and me together and will lead us all back to the Heartwood. See . . . ?"

"See what?" asked Tilly.

"I don't see anything," said Henry.

And there was nothing to see. Because neither of them had it. In the excitement over the discovery of their friends, Mona and Hood had let go of the twine!

"I . . . I can't believe it!" Mona's heart felt heavy in her chest.

"Search!" hollered Hood. "It must be right around here."

But the snow had either buried it or the wind

had blown it away, because the twine was nowhere to be seen.

Mona really *couldn't* believe it. How could she have let go of it? So much for her idea! So much for saving the day! To have found Tilly and Henry only to be lost with them.

She glanced at her friend, huddled beside Henry. Both were shivering in the blanket, the wind whipping their whiskers this way and that. They looked half-frozen.

Mona HAD to find the twine. She peered into the whiteness ahead. It had to be there. It had to!

But there was nothing. Just the endless white, white, white of the snow in front of her. . . .

And yet, could it be? A flash of colorful gold.

It was the twine.

Not lying on the ground, or whipping in the wind, but clutched in the gloved paw of Duchess Hazeline herself! Mona couldn't believe her eyes.

Behind the Duchess was her bright red sleigh, pulled by Francis the fawn, and piled with Gilles, all bundled up, Mrs. Higgins, and a host of others.

"Well, it's about time we caught up to you!" she said. "About time, indeed."

Mona would never have thought she could be so happy to see the Duchess, but she was.

There is a saying in Fernwood Forest that you can only get three bad nuts in a row, which means that only so many things can go wrong before things start to go right.

And at last things were going right.

Mona and Hood had been out a lot longer than they had thought, going in circles, and Mr. Heartwood had begun to worry. He wanted to find Mona and Hood—and Tilly and Henry—but he didn't want to lose anyone else doing so. That's when the Duchess, surprising them all, offered her sleigh. The sleigh was perfect, for it could not only carry them home, but carry home some of the food, too.

Although the Duchess stood awkwardly to the side, seemingly unsure what to do now, Francis was only too eager to help, pulling the sleigh alongside the shipment to make it easier to load. Even the snow was cooperating, the blizzard starting to abate.

Once the sleigh was piled with the crates, they began to sled back to the Heartwood, using the twine as a guide.

"I would have pulled you before if someone had come outside to get me," called Francis. "I'm great at pulling! I told you! Really I am!"

"You really are!" said Mona, as she took a seat with Tilly and Henry at the front, perched on one of the crates of seedcakes. She felt on top of the world, bundled in a blanket, with her friend by her side.

Henry must have, too, because he began to sing joyfully: *"This is the way we brush our tails. . . ."*

"Not that song again!" groaned Tilly.

"What about this one," Mona suggested, and she began:

"Heartwood Hotel, Heartwood Hotel,
Where feathered and furred together can dwell . . ."

This time, Hood didn't tell her to save her voice. Instead Mona noticed his paw tapping along. Soon enough, they could see the Heartwood. The snow was falling more lightly now, and through it, the Heartwood's little windows glimmered, like stars in the distance.

"Do you know," Tilly whispered, between songs, "I think sledding is better than skating."

And even though she had only ever slipped and not skated, Mona agreed.

THE St. BRIGHT EYES BRUNCH

Back at the Heartwood, Mona, Tilly, Hood, and Henry were greeted with a round of cheers. Although no one said anything, Mona could tell that Hood was now more of a hero than a thief in everyone's eyes. Soon the four of them, and a host of others, were curled up by the fire with freshly toasted seedcakes and mugs of hot honey as a snack.

Stacked in a corner of the lobby were boxes from the Beetles' Bed and Boudoir Co., which the carpenter ants were eagerly opening. They were the furniture for the bugs' suites, and part of the squirrels' shipment.

The main shipment, the food, had been carried downstairs to the storage room and some to the kitchen. Ms. Prickles was busy with Maggie and Maurice and others, baking and cooking up a feast, the best brunch the Heartwood had ever seen. A brunch to feed the guests, the orphans, and even the hibernators, who were too excited to fall back asleep.

Mona offered to help, but Ms. Prickles insisted she stay by Tilly's side, to make sure the squirrel was okay.

Tilly was more than okay. She was already grumping.

"I can't believe the hibernators are up. We'll have to get all the day-rooms ready, and it hasn't even stopped snowing yet!"

As though in answer, Francis called in through an upstairs window, "Snow's barely falling!" His voice echoed down the staircase.

"Do you think he'll give us a ride in the sleigh?"

asked the orphan rabbit. "Henry got one. It isn't fair."

"It *was* really fun," said Henry.

"It's not ours. It's the Duchess's," said Hood.

"Did I hear my name?" came the Duchess's voice. She emerged from the staircase, this time not in her nightwear, or bundled up, but wearing her glittery scarf and beautiful long gloves. Despite the finery, there was a new softness about her. Mona could see it.

"Ooo, she's so pretty," sighed the rabbit. "Can I touch your scarf? Can I?"

"Are you a princess?" asked her twin.

"Princess? Oh no. I'm a Duchess. Duchess Hazeline. Everyone knows. . . ." But then she stopped herself. "But I am flattered. And yes, you may touch my scarf." Even so, the Duchess seemed bewildered when the rabbits actually did bound up to do so.

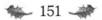

"Here, why don't you take it and try it on," she said, handing it to them.

"Ooo," said one. "Now *I'm* like a princess."

"No, a *duchess*," said the other.

The Duchess seemed even more bewildered. "My goodness," she began, but she was interrupted by Francis.

"Only a few flakes now!"

"Looks like the snow might stop completely," said Hood. "But we couldn't have waited."

"Yeah," said Henry. "I was going to DIE."

"You were singing a song, Henry. Don't exaggerate," said Tilly.

"I'm not!" said Henry.

The porcupine came puffing down the staircase. "I found the games room! Come quick! Come quick!" He turned and ran, puffing back up the stairs.

In a flurry, the orphans joined him—even Henry and the little rabbits who were arguing over who was going to wear the scarf.

With the orphans gone, the lobby became quiet. The fire crackled. A tiny bed squeaked as the ants pulled it from its packaging. Mona munched on a toasty seedcake. Delicious smells were beginning to drift down the hallway from the ballroom— crab apple puffs, acorn soufflé, and even cheese crumble.

"I *had* planned to wear that scarf at the conference," said the Duchess, taking a seat on the couch that they left empty. She sighed. "Of course that was before. . . ."

"Before what, Duchess?" Mona asked, nibbling her seedcake.

"Before I found out there was no conference."

Mona gulped her bite. So that was why the Duchess was in no hurry to leave; why Francis said he was taking her back to her home.

"Well, there *was* a conference—but not at my warren," the Duchess went on. "This year, the organizers chose another warren. So, of course, I refused to attend. I have the most beautiful burrow in all the forests far and wide, and yet . . . I just don't understand it. . . ." The Duchess sniffed. But it wasn't a snobby sniff. It was a sad one. "Well, perhaps that's not being honest. Perhaps I do understand. I haven't always been, shall we say, the easiest to get along with. I am only ever trying to be helpful, you know. It's not my fault other animals aren't raised as well as I . . ."

Tilly humphed but didn't say anything.

The Duchess continued. "I've always had the best of everything. The best governesses, the best food, the best warren. Still, sometimes the best is rather . . . lonely. It turns out my warren is rather big for a single rabbit. And so I came to the Heartwood. I knew I would find company. And I did, in a manner of speaking. Yet I was still alone."

"But you have so many admirers," said Tilly.

"Yes, but not friends," said the Duchess. And Mona gave Tilly's paw a squeeze.

The Duchess nodded upon seeing that gesture. "It was that—seeing what you would do for one another—that changed me. I was alone, but I didn't have to be. I could choose to join in and help. Instead of driving others away, I could bring them together."

"It was good you did," said Hood.

And, instead of her usual sniff, this time the Duchess smiled.

Hood smiled, too.

And suddenly, Mona had an idea. The Duchess

had such a big burrow—a big lonely burrow—and Hood and his orphans had no home. It could be the perfect pairing. . . .

No one had a chance to hear her thought, though, because they were interrupted by an incredible sight. It was Mr. Heartwood. He was dressed up again. But instead of his pajamas, he was wearing a hat that looked like an upside-down tulip and was carrying a large bell. He looked ridiculous! Mona couldn't help but giggle.

Ding-da-ding-da-ding! Mr. Heartwood rang the bell. *Ding-da-ding-da-ding!*

Moments later, the orphans scrambled down the stairs.

"St. Bright Eyes! It's St. Bright Eyes!" cried Henry.

"No, it's . . ." started Mona.

But Tilly shushed her. "Yep, it's St. Bright Eyes."

"But St. Bright Eyes never comes when it's still snowing!" cried Henry.

"Well, I guess this year is different," said Tilly.

"St. Bright Eyes is here! To spread warm wishes and holiday cheer!" bellowed Mr. Heartwood.

The orphans crowded around him as he led them into the dining room. Mona heard shouts of amazement.

"A WHOLE pond of honey!"

"There REALLY is one!"

"And look!"

The bells rang again and Mr. Heartwood—St. Bright Eyes—bellowed, "Now, now, now! Brunch will only begin once you all settle in."

"That must mean us, too," said the Duchess, and she stood up and headed into the dining hall, followed by Hood and the others. Mona watched them talking as they went. She would suggest her plan later. But Tilly was lingering, and Mona wanted to stay with her friend.

"Sheesh! Henry sure has a lot of energy, huh?" said Tilly. "So much for our quiet winter."

Mona nodded. It had definitely *not* been a quiet winter. But she wouldn't have it any other way. Busy was better—if it meant making new friends and having new adventures.

"I wonder if Mr. Heartwood will let Henry stay here. Do you think?" Tilly continued. "He's rhyming again, so that's good."

Mona was about to say she was sure he would let Henry stay there, but she stopped. She didn't want to make any promises that weren't hers to make. "I bet so," she said instead. "You know how nice Mr. Heartwood is. Hood's nice, too, isn't he? Even if he *was* the thief. . . ."

"About that," said Tilly. "I'm sorry I blamed you. . . ."

"No, I'm sorry," said Mona quickly. "I shouldn't have kept a secret. . . ."

"Pish-posh, haven't you figured that out by

now? The Heartwood Hotel is ALWAYS full of secrets."

"I think you're right," said Mona.

"Of course I'm right," said Tilly. "Now come on, we'd better hurry up if we want to hear St. Bright Eyes's song. It's so funny. And maybe Mr. Heartwood will even juggle the pea pods again. The St. Bright Eyes Brunch is the best. It's even better than St. Slumber's Supper. I mean, St. Slumber's Supper is pretty great, with the gifts and everything, but at the St. Bright Eyes Brunch you get to crack open a seed and find your fortune for spring. Mr. Gibson writes them! And they're always good—" She paused. "Well, interesting."

"But who is St. Bright Eyes?" asked Mona.

"Oh, of course," said Tilly. "That's St. Slumber's best friend."

Tilly smiled, and Mona smiled back.

And with that, they got up from their cozy spots by the fire. But before they left the lobby,

Mona gave it one last glance. There was no rug at the Heartwood door and the floor was muddy, covered in prints and small pools of snowy water shaped like flowers.

But as messy as it was, it didn't matter. Because the important things were there. The crackling fire, the smell of good food, and a friend holding her paw.

And as long as she had those things, Mona knew, she was ready for whatever secrets—and surprises—the spring might bring.

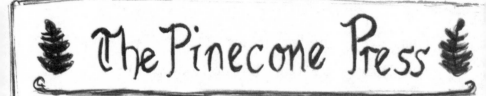

The Pinecone Press

Fernwood's Orphans Find a Home

The famed Duchess Hazeline has just announced the opening of a brand-new orphan-age in Fernwood Forest. This much-needed center for the care and protection of young orphaned animals will be located in her newly renovated warren. Duchess Hazeline will jointly share the position of Head of Programs with William Hood, who has been in charge of a smaller operation over the past few years.

This new center has the facilities and staff to accommo-date more than thirty young animals.

"We have dark rooms for moles and bats, swings for opossums, fur-lined burrows for baby bunnies, and mud boxes for frogs," the Duchess says. "I was inspired to open the home during my recent stay at the Heartwood Hotel, at which time I was involved in a rescue of orphaned animals during this winter's blizzard." (For more on the Bad, Bad Blizzard, see page 2.)

The grand opening of the home will take place tomorrow afternoon in Mossy Square, with music provided by Cybele and the Dove Tones, and complimentary refreshments from the Heartwood Hotel.

Remember, when you see a young animal in need, please send a messenger jay or visit Hood & Hazeline's Home for Orphaned Animals.

IN OTHER NEWS: The Heartwood Hotel reveals its bug-sized renovations!

Acknowledgments

I am lucky to be gifted with such great family, friends, and colleagues, who help me write the best books I can. Thank you to my dad, mom, brother, and Marie, and my grandparents, who watch over me; as well as my friends, including the Inkslingers (Tanya Lloyd Kyi, Rachelle Delaney, Christy Goezern, Shannon Ozirny, Lori Sherritt-Fleming, and Maryn Quarless), Lee Edward Fodi, Sara Gillingham, and Vikki Vansickle. Thank you to my amazing editors Rotem Moscovich and Suzanne Sutherland, and to the fantastic teams at Disney-Hyperion and HarperCollins Canada, and to the brilliant artist Stephanie Graegin. Thank you to my wonderful agent, Emily van Beek; my dear husband, Luke Spence Byrd; and the incredible Tiffany Stone, who practically lives at the Heartwood Hotel with me when I'm writing about it.

*Turn the page for a sneak peek at Mona's next
adventure at the Heartwood Hotel!*

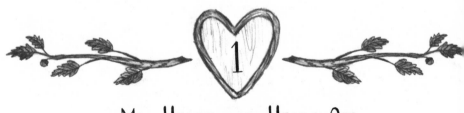

MR. HEARTWOOD HEADS OFF

There was a buzz in the air at the Heartwood Hotel. Mona the mouse could feel it in her whiskers. It was spring, and the guests, staff, and even the tree itself were beginning to buzz with activity. Buds were bursting on the branches, sap seeped from the bark, and the floors had a bounce to them. There was even a *real* buzz, too: from the bees, who had been hired to make honey for the guests.

The only one who wasn't full of energy was Mr. Heartwood, the hotel's owner. Winter had been unusually eventful, and the great badger had been dragging his paws ever since. So, at last, with much encouragement from everyone, he was going to take a break and visit a friend.

All the staff were gathered in the lobby to see him off. It was like check-out—a really grand one.

Mona smoothed her maid's apron, making sure to look presentable, and straightened the key around her neck.

For once, Mr. Heartwood wasn't wearing his own keys or his vest. Instead he sported a cardigan and a cap. Beside him was his suitcase, made of a burl with roots for handles. Mona had seen all sorts of suitcases in the hotel, from tiny seeds to hollow branches. His was the biggest.

But Mr. Heartwood wasn't picking it up. He was still trying to run the hotel.

"Is the spring cleaning . . ."

"Sorted and started, Mr. Heartwood," said Mrs. Higgins, the hedgehog head housekeeper.

"And the food . . ."

"Stocked and stored, Mr. Heartwood. We just

got a shipment," said Ms. Prickles, the porcupine cook.

"What of bookings . . ."

"We're low so far this season . . ." started Mrs. Higgins.

"But don't worry," interrupted Gilles, the front-desk lizard. He would be in charge while Mr. Heartwood was away. "The Hop is coming, and I have plans to spruce it up."

"What's the Hop?" Mona whispered to Tilly.

"A big party—sort of like the Acorn Festival," Tilly whispered back.

Tilly the squirrel was not only Mona's best friend, but also the head maid, as well as the best grumper in the whole of the Heartwood. But lately she'd been grinning more than grumping, ever since she'd found Henry, her long-lost little brother.

"I love parties!" said Henry loudly. Henry had a *very* loud voice.

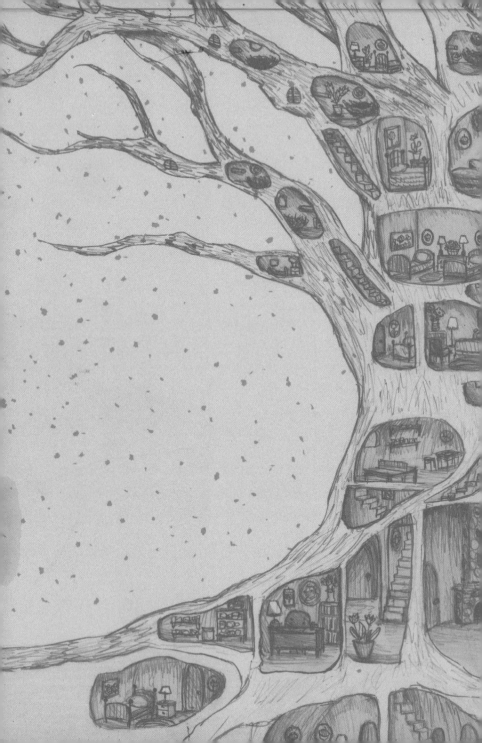